ABOUT THE AUTHOR

Jim Anotsu has been writing since he was ten years old. As well as being a huge Minecraft fan, he loves rapping, painting and writing music. He lives with his wife and a one-eyed cat called January.

Other books by Jim Anotsu:

The Sword of Herobrine:
An unofficial Minecraft-fan adventure

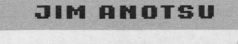

HEROBRINE'S REVENGE

PUFFIN

PUFFIN BOOKS

UK | USA | Canada | Ireland | Australia
India | New Zealand | South Africa

Puffin Books is part of the Penguin Random House group of companies
whose addresses can be found at global.penguinrandomhouse.com.

www.penguin.co.uk
www.puffin.co.uk
www.ladybird.co.uk

Originally published in the Portuguese language in Brazil by Editora Nemo, 2016
English-language edition first published in Great Britain by Puffin Books, 2016

001

Typeset in 12/19 pt Sabon
Printed in Great Britain by Clays Ltd, St Ives plc

A CIP catalogue record for this book is available from the British Library

ISBN: 978-0-141-37375-1

All correspondence to
Puffin Books
Penguin Random House Children's
80 Strand, London WC2R 0RL

For my friends – you know who you are.

The road is us.

CONTENTS

PART 1

THE GIRL AND
THE PIXELS

CHAPTER 1

THE NEW TRAIL

Some people like chocolate. Some people like rap. Some people like getting up early on Sundays (crazy, I know). But me, I liked games. *League of Legends*, *World of Warcraft*, *DotA* . . . I played them all, but Minecraft had always been my favourite. Hour after hour I spent building houses, killing monsters and searching for food. It might not seem that cool to some people, but it was undeniably addictive. And it was my addiction to the Overworld that led me to where I ended up – but I guess I'd better start at the beginning . . .

It was a standard day – I ran out of school and rushed down the road so I could get home in five minutes and play for a bit before dinner. I travelled up in our building's lift, walked into the flat, grabbed something from the fridge and then ran to the computer in my bedroom. Behind me, I heard my mother yell at me for leaving my stuff on the floor.

'Bia,' said my mum when she came in to see me. 'Dinner is ready. Don't be long.'

I nodded. 'Just five minutes, please!'

I always spent more than five minutes playing – if I didn't play then, I wouldn't get another chance until way later, because after dinner I had to do my homework. The problem with being thirteen years old is that you're so close to being independent and getting to do what you like, but at the same time you're still *so* far away. It's like an armadillo stretching its arms out to try to touch the moon.

OK, maybe that isn't the best simile ever, but it should give you an idea of how I felt about adolescence.

I took off my school shirt and pulled on a worn-out Linkin Park t-shirt. As soon as my computer turned on I entered the game, crossing my fingers that no griefer had destroyed my constructions. That was the biggest threat to the digital world: griefers, the people who spent all their time messing up other people's games, destroying everything they had built. In the past few days, griefers had been causing havoc – players had been complaining the world over, but not even the game's creators seemed to have an answer as to what was going on.

'Please, Minecraft,' I muttered. 'In the name of Father Notch, don't let my castle have been destroyed.'

Minecraft servers had been hit hard lately. Entire map areas had been annihilated, hordes of monsters that players couldn't fight against had been appearing, and Nether portals were popping up everywhere. It was even worse than that time when a griefer who called himself the Red King had tried to rule the Overworld.

Fortunately, none of my things had been damaged since I last entered the game – the castle I was building with ten towers and hundreds of tunnels was still standing, and so was the enclosure I built for sheep and cows, and my beautiful waterfall.

There was a creeper prowling about my house, but that was to be expected, and I could finish off that green thing in no time at all.

Everything seemed all right in my digital world. The character I played was looking after the land and the animals – it seemed like an ordinary day in the Overworld.

I say 'seemed' because, right then, everything changed.

The computer screen froze, and nothing I tried made it go back to normal again. At first I thought it was some kind of hardware glitch, but then the screen turned all green and a long sequence of numbers flashed up – zeros and ones spreading out endlessly in front of my eyes.

'Mum, did you mess with the router?' I shouted at the top of my lungs.

I bashed the CPU several times, but no luck. I pressed every key, but it didn't help.

Then, just as I was about to pull the plug out and put a stop to it altogether, the green light from the screen glowed even brighter, filling the whole of my bedroom and forcing me to shut my eyes. It felt like one of the longest moments of my life. Everything seemed to happen in slow motion. It was as though I was swimming against a current, and I could feel my body being dragged under.

I screamed.

The horror movie continued. My hands tried to find something to hold on to, but an invisible force pulled me and wouldn't let go. I was engulfed by that glowing green sea; everything turned dark, and then I couldn't feel anything at all.

THE OVERWORLD

By Punk-Princess166

The Overworld's blocks are as real as the earth, stones and grass in the normal world. It's easy to be misled and think that the pixelated creatures that roam about the Overworld aren't actually alive, but that would be a mistake.

In the Overworld, the sun rises, shines, sets . . . then the moon rises.

And, with it, the monsters rise too.

It's crucial that you've rested and eaten well by the time the moon is high in the sky because it brings all kinds of night-time creatures to knock on your door.

When you're in the Overworld, you don't need hammers or nails, sanders or saws to make anything. All you need to do is put the raw materials on a crafting table in the right sequence and combination, and you can build anything as simple as a bowl or as complex as a brewing stand.

Most of the key things you need – iron, coal, gold, diamond – can be found deep in certain rocks. You can use these materials to create new things or build swords and armour to fight against the greatest dangers that the darkness brings.

During the day, life can be calm and peaceful in the Overworld – you can rear cows, plant crops, make cakes and collect eggs. A well-prepared player is a happy player. But, to be well prepared, first you'll have to handle a serious number of challenges and dangers.

CHAPTER 2

THE NEW WORLD

That was how it all began. My eyes started to get used to the light; the heat of the sun warmed my skin; there was an earthy taste in my mouth. I didn't have the slightest idea as to how I had ended up wherever I now was, but I could tell that this was going to be the start of a dangerous adventure.

I got up, still confused, and faced the world before me: blocky shapes stretched out to the horizon over contours that I had seen many times before on my computer screen. The trees, the rocks, the animals, and even the sun above my head . . . I recognized them all. I didn't have a clue how I'd got there, I didn't know how to get back or whether I ever would – but I was certain of one thing. I was in the Overworld.

I stared at the woods near by, grateful not to have arrived in the middle of a forest or at night when monsters would be roaming about – especially as I didn't even have a wooden sword. Appearing in a good biome was a positive start. I guess in that sense luck was on my side.

I had no idea what time it was or how soon night would fall, so I began to walk around aimlessly, trying to find shelter. I knew that was the key: finding a place to hide from the creatures that would come out at nightfall. After wandering for a while to get my bearings, I took a deep breath and turned to walk towards the sun. Everything seemed all right so far, but I had a bad feeling that things were going to change soon.

I thought back to how I had ended up there – the numbers on the computer screen, the green light, that peculiar feeling of being dragged under. I wonder if my mum had heard me screaming. If she had, no doubt she would be making a fuss back home – calling the police and things. I decided to find a way back to my world as quickly as possible.

I walked for about half an hour towards the sun. It had already begun to drop lower in the sky, which had me worried. As I walked, I picked some fruit to eat – it tasted sugary and left my tongue numb for a second after I swallowed. But, bearing in mind it was digital food, I guess it wasn't too bad. I was just biting into an apple when I heard a voice swearing from somewhere to my left.

I wasn't alone.

I threw the apple away and moved towards the voice; as I followed the sound I heard another noise from the same direction. It sounded like a laser in a sci-fi film. I trod carefully and quietly, trying to work out whether this person was a friend or a foe. I bent to pick up a stone from the ground – a pretty pathetic weapon, but it was better than no weapon at all. As I drew nearer, the noises grew louder and more distinct. Ahead of me was a sharp drop down the side of a very steep hill; I approached the edge and looked down to see what was happening below.

A boy – as human as I was – stood at the bottom of the hill, far below. He wore a pair of jeans and a red hoodie, and he held in his hand a large iron sword. He was weilding it against his enemy – a giant purple-eyed creature with long arms. This monster would frighten pretty much any Minecraft player: it was an enderman. The battle was fierce, and the hooded boy handled his sword with great skill, delivering several blows as he dodged the claws at the end of those long arms.

I watched as the boy sliced with his sword and cut off one of the creature's arms. The monster wailed in pain and teleported away. But the boy chased after the enderman, charging fiercely and mercilessly. The monster tried to retreat, but it was weak and its teleportation powers seemed to be failing.

Then, suddenly, the creature disappeared again. I waited for it to emerge once more, even closer to the boy in the red hoodie, but it didn't. I heard the distinctive noise it made – as if a giant whip had lashed in the air – and then I knew. The enderman was right behind me.

I turned and saw those purple eyes glowing like fire, the creature's remaining arm stretching forward as it tried to get hold of me. I shouted the nastiest word I could think of and spun round to try and escape, but I was already losing hope.

I tripped and fell down the sharp drop, my body crashing into the wet ground all the way down the hill and hitting every stone hard. Hoping against all hope I wasn't breaking any bones, I screamed at the top of my lungs as my body rolled all the way to the bottom. It happened so fast that I felt sick and dizzy.

I swore when I reached the bottom. 'Next time,' I grumbled, 'I'm taking the lift.'

Although I couldn't see it from where I lay, I could tell that the enderman had teleported again, this time to right in front of the kid in the red hoodie. Now though, it seemed like the boy had the advantage – he thrust his sword forward and attacked the monster. I was still dizzy and confused; I couldn't see what happened next all that clearly, but I did manage to spot the monster's head as it fell to the ground and rolled past me, leaving the earth stained with blood.

I tried to stand up and say something, but I felt so sick I couldn't bring myself to move. The mysterious boy walked over to the enderman and thrust his sword into the creature's chest, then kneeled and stuck his hand inside, searching for something. I guessed what he was looking for, and watched as he pulled out a big pearl, an ender pearl. That was what gave the enderman most of its powers, and it was a real treasure in the hands of any player.

Only then did the kid turn towards me. He was a golden-haired boy with bright, moonlike eyes. But his face lacked expression; he looked like the kind of person who never smiled.

I opened my mouth to try and say something, but after my fall all I could manage was a pathetic attempt at a smile before, all of a sudden, I threw up everything in my stomach.

It wasn't a pretty sight.

CHAPTER 3

ENCOUNTERS IN THE OVERWORLD

It took me a full minute to manage to stand up. My head ached and my arms were dirty and scratched all over. The hooded kid stood motionless, just staring. Once he realized I was done throwing up, he stepped forward and spoke to me.

'You're a User too,' he said, in a cold, calm voice. 'How did you get here? Is there anybody else with you?'

'No,' I replied. 'I haven't got a clue how I ended up here. I was playing Minecraft at home and now . . . Here I am!'

He drew a piece of cloth from his pocket and wiped both the sword and the ender pearl clean, then put the pearl in a rucksack which lay near by. He must have thrown his bag aside before the battle. He was very neat; every move he made seemed pre-planned.

'You're lucky to have appeared here and not somewhere else,' he said. 'Much of the Overworld has already been destroyed by Herobrine and his henchmen.'

I laughed in confusion. 'Herobrine?' I said. 'Everyone knows he's an urban legend. People just made him up to frighten off new players.'

'Most people don't believe it'd be possible to fall into a digital world,' the boy answered. 'And yet here we are. Herobrine is real, and he's worse than you could have ever imagined. He's like a machine bent on destroying everything.'

The boy was right – after everything that had just happened, and all the things I'd just seen, it didn't make sense for me to simply assume Herobrine wasn't real. But, if he did exist, that would be the worst possible news. I knew Herobrine's story, how he was the creature all players feared, how he would watch players, corrupting everything in his way, controlling monsters and turning even the gentlest creatures into killers.

'Is that why there have been problems with the game on the other side?' I asked. 'Hordes of monsters? Nether portals opening and parts of the map that just disappear?'

The boy didn't answer. He slung his rucksack on his back and began to walk away. I had no better option so I followed him. He didn't complain, so I figured he didn't mind.

The sky was turning a reddish colour, a sign it would soon be nightfall – by then we really needed to be in a safe place.

'Ah, so the other side has already begun to suffer,' the boy murmured, as though he was speaking more to himself than to me. 'The area where people play Minecraft is just at the edge of the Overworld. We're deep inside it, at the bottom of it all, so if players are already feeling the impact . . . it means we're running out of time.'

After walking for a while, the grass beneath our feet turned into an expanse of stone that stretched far out of sight. There were no trees or animals here – just the devastated land, covered with the bones of many mobs who had died there. The kid told me all of this was Herobrine's work, and many years ago there had been a village full of Steves here – ordinary, hardworking people who had been wiped out of the Overworld. All that was left were bones, which, for one reason or another, hadn't been turned into pixels.

I put my hands in my pockets and asked a question that had been troubling me for a while. 'And what if Herobrine can make it all the way to that edge you mentioned? The place where people play Minecraft?'

'Then he will win,' the boy replied. 'Herobrine doesn't just want to rule over the Overworld – as soon as his work is done here, he'll sneak into the rest of the internet, and each and every bit of the digital world will be his. Do you see how serious this is?'

I did. I saw it all. The real world was connected through cables, data and networks – everybody's life was linked to the internet. I thought back to the time when a national security agent told the world that his government spied on everyone through the internet, eavesdropping and recording everything they did. I could hardly imagine what Herobrine would do if he had that sort of power. If he achieved his aim, everything would be under his control, from telephones to nuclear missiles. We would all be in serious trouble.

'Is there any way we can defeat him?' I asked.

'I've been trying for years,' the boy answered. 'I hope I'll find a way. Otherwise we'll all be lost.'

We walked in silence as I mulled over what he had said. Everything seemed a lot more frightening now. I wasn't just playing a computer game – now I knew that if Herobrine managed to escape, everything would suffer: my family, my city, my school and my life. For the first time since I had arrived in the Overworld, I wished I was back home.

'This is it,' the kid said. He kneeled down and carefully removed a stone; beneath it was a well-lit staircase spiralling endlessly down. 'This is my hiding place,' he said. 'At least for now. Let's go. I've got some food down there.'

'That's exactly what I need,' I said.

The sky was almost black by now. Stars began to appear in the sky, and I could hear distant noises of monsters all around. I shivered and headed down the stairs. Behind me my travel companion put the stone back in place to hide the entrance. The stairway was as silent as a tomb then and, when the boy next spoke, it sounded loud and ominous, although he barely raised his voice above a whisper.

'By the way,' he said, 'my name is Vincent.'

CHAPTER 4

CONVERSATIONS BENEATH
THE SURFACE

At the bottom of the stairs was a large room containing a couple of sofas and beds, a wooden table and an array of different kinds of weapons in every corner, as though this kid was getting ready for a war. I spotted swords, shields, bows, axes and some other weapons I'd never seen in the game. Vincent said that this was just one of his bases, a place to rest before he carried on fighting against Herobrine.

'And who are you, User?' he asked as he put some vegetables in the oven. 'You might as well fill me in – I suspect we're going to be here for a while.'

I sat on one of the sofas and stretched out my legs. 'My name is Bianca, but everyone calls me

Bia,' I said. 'I'm just another girl hooked on video games and manga. Tell me about yourself – Vincent is an interesting name.'

'My mother's a painter,' he replied. 'Vincent van Gogh was her favourite artist, that's why I'm called Vincent.'

I nodded, staring around the room of this strange boy named after the famous painter. 'Do you know if there's any way to get out of here?' I asked. 'I mean, to get back to the real world? Although I guess if you knew a way, you would've gone back already.'

He smiled. Or rather, one corner of his mouth twitched a little. 'I know two people who managed to leave this place and go back home. Two Users who came here before you – Noobie Saibot and Punk-Princess166, they were called,' he said. 'But they could only escape from here because Herobrine was scared of them – he sent them away.'

A wave of adrenalin surged through my body. Other humans had already been here and made it back home! 'So Herobrine is afraid of someone?' I said. 'Maybe we should try to send a message to them.'

Vincent served the vegetables on to two plates and put them on the table with some boiled eggs and two glasses of water. 'Herobrine is scared of any User,' he answered. 'You and I are both a threat to him, and I'm sure he already knows you're here. But the fact you *are* here means we might have a chance to save our world by fighting against him.'

I said nothing, concentrating on eating the potatoes and carrots on my plate. I could hear noises coming from the ground above – creepers blowing up, endermen and zombies searching for food, the howl of werewolves. It must have been the dead of night by then; a lot of monsters would have emerged. I couldn't help thinking how absurd it was to believe someone like me could challenge someone like Herobrine. Just hearing the monsters above us scared me to death – how was I going to face someone with such evil powers?

'I don't think I can help you,' I said at last. 'I'm really good at playing on the other side of the screen, using a keyboard and a mouse, but I've never fought with a sword in my life before, so I don't think I'm going to be any use.'

Vincent put his fork down on the table and looked at me for a while before answering. 'That's what I thought when I got here, but then I learned that the monsters are more scared of us than we are of them.' He paused as a blast rang out from the ground above us. 'Everything here has been created by humans – every mob, every biome. They look upon us as gods, so we have the power to destroy them.'

Just for a second, I saw a gleam in his eyes – they were the eyes of someone who had already been in hundreds of battles, the eyes of someone who had been alone for far too long. I saw, too, something murky hidden behind them, something he was trying hard to conceal. The truth was, I knew very little about this person sitting across the table from me. I'd been so relieved to find a human in this strange world that so far I'd been trusting him blindly.

'Do you really think you can defeat Herobrine?' I asked. 'Just you on your own in the middle of nowhere, with an iron sword?'

'I'm going to defeat him,' Vincent said, his voice low. 'Even if it's the last thing I ever do, Bia. There's a legend I believe will be the key to his defeat – all I need is to find someone who has a record of the legend in full. If I had that, I could defeat him.' He paused and scratched his head. 'I'm tired, and tomorrow is going to be a long day. There's a duvet on the other bed – help yourself. Goodnight.'

I remained silent, staring at the plate he'd left on the table. Vincent sat on his bed and picked up a book with a worn-out cover. I realized I'd upset him – withdrawing into silence was his way of closing the whole conversation before I brought anything else up. My new friend was a mystery to me, but tonight wasn't the time to find further answers to the questions in my mind.

I finished eating my vegetables and then dropped into bed myself, dead tired. In no time my heavy eyelids began to shut. Drifting far away, I began to dream.

CONCEPTS OF THE OVERWORLD

WHAT HAPPENS AT NIGHT

By Punk-Princess166

In the Overworld, night belongs to the dead, not the living – it belongs to the creatures from the abyss. Yeah, that sounds awful, but it's a pretty accurate summary of what happens after nightfall in the Overworld.

The first thing you need to do when you appear – some people call it spawning, emerging or starting, but those are just different words to describe the moment you first turn up somewhere on the map – is to brace yourself for the night ahead. I don't mean heating up some mushroom soup or finding some woolly blankets. I mean getting yourself a torch, some shelter and a sword.

There is nothing as scary as finding yourself alone in the dead of night with nowhere to hide. Or, even if you do find somewhere to hide, not having a torch to light your shelter. Being in the dark, being unable to see even what's right in front of your eyes, hearing zombies moaning, spiders' legs clacking and skeletons' bones rattling . . . it's a horrible experience.

The moon will become a constant presence in your life, and sunset will no longer be beautiful – it will be frightening. Only the strongest and best prepared will ever enjoy gazing at the orange evening sky as it shifts into black, starry night.

CHAPTER 5

LEAVING THE CAVE

The morning started gently. I opened my eyes and smelled coffee. I wasn't even a fan of coffee, but anything that reminded me of home would do, whether it was a smell or a taste. For a few minutes I lay there, mesmerized by that fabulous coffee smell, then I looked round and saw Vincent putting two cups and a cake on the table.

'Good morning,' he said. 'I hope you feel better today. I must continue my journey – the place I'm looking for is a temple relatively near by, and it might be my last chance to defeat Herobrine. I want to take advantage of the daylight to cover as much ground as I can.'

Getting up, I realized I had slept with my shoes

on. My All Stars, once perfectly white, were now covered in mud. I dragged myself out of bed towards the table and sat down to have some coffee and a slice of cake. The cake was the sweetest thing I had ever tasted, but that wasn't a problem for me – I definitely have a sweet tooth. The coffee tasted like a cat had died in it, so I really hoped that Vincent never had to earn his living as a barista.

'I'll do anything if it'll help me get back home,' I said. 'Except for having another cup of your coffee. It's absolutely horrible.'

Vincent smiled, a tiny, quick smile that soon vanished. He pushed his golden hair back from his face. 'I don't like my coffee either,' he said, shrugging and then strapping his rucksack on. 'It's never going to taste good when you have to use an old sock as a coffee strainer.'

The coffee tasted even bitterer in my throat now, and I seriously considered throwing up. Vincent was unreadable – it was impossible to work out whether he was telling the truth or joking. I prayed that it was a bad joke. Or rather, I decided to believe it had been just a joke, otherwise . . . well, that would account for the dead-cat taste I'd already noticed. 'I hope that was a joke,' I told him. 'It'd better be, or else Herobrine will be the least of your worries.'

The boy stared at me for a moment. When he answered, his tone was serious. 'I think we have more important things to talk about, Bianca.'

'Bia,' I corrected him.

'I think we have more important things to talk about, *Bia*.' He grabbed his sword and handed me one of my own before he left. I heard his footsteps on the stairs as he ran up them.

'I won't forget about this, all right?' I shouted after him. 'As soon as we finish kicking that evil Herobrine's butt, we're going to have a serious talk about that coffee.'

I followed him up the stairs and into the sunlight that was already touching the Overworld's surface. All around us were remains from the monsters' attacks, the bones and pixels that were all that was left of those who had been too silly or slow to find shelter. The random appearance of monsters was one of the main features of the game – as long as there was a bit of shade, monsters could spawn out of nowhere. This was just a cool feature of Minecraft when I was on the other side of the computer. But, here, it was a nightmare. As I thought about monsters spawning, something else crossed my mind. I moved across the huge expanse of stony ground to stand next to Vincent.

'I've got a question,' I said. 'What happens if I die here? I mean, I guess people just reappear somewhere else when they die?'

Vincent stood still, twisting the point of his sword on the ground. 'You just die,' he said eventually. 'It's that simple. People like us don't re-emerge anywhere – we aren't like the mobs on your screen. Unfortunately, we only have one chance to get it right. So, if you died here, back in our world you'd just be some girl who went missing and was never found.'

We began to walk along those lifeless plains where no trees grew, pacing over the hot ground and staring out at the desolate landscape. I couldn't think of anything except the fact that I *had* to survive the Overworld, no matter what. I plodded along through that stone desert in silence, step by step, thinking that being sucked into my favourite game hadn't turned out well at all. I tried to find comfort in the thought that at least I wasn't inside *The Last of Us* or *WoW*, where I would definitely be dead by now. But not even that idea helped relieve the cold feeling in my stomach.

'Don't worry, Bia,' Vincent said. 'I won't let you die. You'll get back home and live until you're ninety.'

I looked up and smiled. 'I hope so,' I said. 'My mother would be really upset if I died before I cleaned up my bedroom.'

Feeling a bit more cheerful now, I kept walking across the hot ground, heading towards the lost temple.

CHAPTER 6

THE RELENTLESS CHASE

Vincent and I walked for about five hours, stopping every now and again to take a break. The stony desert was far bigger than I'd thought – it stretched for several kilometres. If Herobrine had devastated this biome in this way, I could only imagine what he was capable of doing to the rest of the world.

Vincent remained silent most of the time, and I realized that was just his way – he spoke rarely and held his sword in his hand at all times. Every so often we came across a tree that hadn't been knocked down, its trunk and square top rising towards the sky. One of these times, we took a break beneath the tree, stopping for some water and a little food.

'We can't stay too long around here,' Vincent said, looking down at the map he'd brought out from his bag. 'We're still about an hour's walk from one of my old shelters. I hope it's still there.'

I stared at him, baffled and upset by the uncertainty in his voice – I'd just been walking for hours under the scorching sun, believing we were heading somewhere safe. 'So you mean you don't know whether your hiding place is still there?' I said. 'We could end up in the middle of nowhere after nightfall!'

'After Herobrine began destroying the Overworld, I lost some bases,' Vincent replied, his eyes still on the map. 'I haven't had a chance to check them all yet, but I don't think he's gone beyond this point. He didn't come here looking for my base – he came here to slay all the Steves.'

'How come you have all these bases around?' I asked. 'You must have been here for a long time to have built so many.'

Vincent shrugged his shoulders. 'According to the calendar of the real world, I've been here about a month,' he replied, still not looking at me. 'According to the calendar of the Overworld, I've been here for many years. Time passes faster here. No one knows why.'

I couldn't help wondering what must have happened to him over all the years he'd been here. Did he not have family on the other side? Why would anyone choose to spend their life inside a digital world when there were real people on the other side of the screen? Perhaps that accounted for his being so quiet most of the time, as well as for that odd gleam in his eyes – maybe they were the eyes of someone who had been alone for so long he'd forgotten how to get on with real people. It dawned on me then that I was probably the first human he had come across in a long time.

I was deep in thought when Vincent tapped me on the shoulder and pointed to a place towards the west – at least, I think it was west.

'We've got some company,' he said. 'Get ready to run!'

I followed the direction of Vincent's gaze and immediately I saw what he meant. A green horde was approaching us, and fast. I could tell a creeper from miles away, but seeing them like this – so many of them packed together in a stampede – was pretty terrifying. The huge pack of box-headed, four-legged creepers loped towards us at high speed. I could hear the usual noise they made, the sound of a burning fuse.

Vincent looked at me, his eyes wide. 'Run!' he shouted.

I did what I was told. I forgot about being tired and ran as fast as I could, hoping we could find a place to hide somewhere near by. Anywhere would do. There were more than fifty creepers chasing after us; I could hear them running fast behind me. In the game, I hated creepers the most – they destroyed everything a player had built just for the sake of it by blowing up. And here they were, proving me right – they *were* the worst monsters. The hatred I felt for them grew.

'They're going to catch up with us!' I shouted.

'They won't as long as we keep on running,' Vincent called back. 'Just run as fast as you can. According to the map, there's a bridge about a kilometre away. All we need to do is to go over the bridge – the creepers can't all get across it at the same time.'

'I hope your map is accurate!' I yelled.

A whole kilometre away! I really regretted being one of the worst students at P.E. back in school – I struggled even to run round the block. Now I needed to run a thousand metres in record time to avoid getting caught and blown up by a pack of green monsters. It was starting to feel like every minute I spent here was an attempt to confirm Murphy's law: anything that can go wrong, will go wrong.

I looked back one last time and saw a massive blast, followed by another and another. One of the monsters had blown up too soon, and the knock-on effect was so powerful I felt a gust of wind strike my face.

Oh, crap, I thought.

CREEPERS

By Punk-Princess166

Creepers are seriously annoying mobs that emerge in the dead of night and don't get killed by the daylight. They usually wander around in woods, hills and forests. They are a real pain in the neck and can even blow up in your face.

Getting rid of one of them is easy. All a warrior has to do is strike the creeper several times, then make sure they're well away before the creeper explodes.

These monsters have caused havoc in the Overworld, damaging houses, gardens, sculptures, crops and even entire biomes – they're the greatest enemy to the landscape.

So whenever you're about to come out of your hiding place, make sure you look out through the window first to avoid any nasty, dangerous and unpleasant encounters.

The gunpowder that stays on your body after the creeper dies can be collected and is very useful, especially for making TNT.

CHAPTER 7

EXPLOSIONS AND CHASES

I had to be brave and run as fast as I could, otherwise I'd be torn to pieces. I told myself all I had to do was keep on running, even if I was out of breath, even if my legs ached all over. I couldn't give up, no matter how much I wished none of this was happening.

'Keep on running,' Vincent called. 'We're nearly there.'

'Yeah, running was my plan!' I shouted back. 'Who wants to be blown up by a creeper?'

'I'm glad to hear that.'

I looked back and realized the horde of creepers was gaining on us. I knew they never got tired, so I tried to run faster.

I could already make out in the distance the shape

of the bridge Vincent had told me about; with each step I took it became more and more distinct. I didn't have the slightest idea what he intended to do once we had crossed over the bridge, but I clung to the glimmer of hope the bridge represented, linking one side to the other.

We got closer. It was an old wooden rope-bridge. The ropes looked pretty worn out. As it swayed, some fragments fell off; it looked like it would collapse as soon as anyone set foot on it.

'You want me to go on that?' I asked Vincent. 'This will kill us faster than any creeper!'

'This is our best chance, Bia,' Vincent replied as he ran.

I sighed and kept on sprinting towards the bridge. I could feel the ground shuddering as the monsters thundered behind us; I could hear the hissing-fuse sound they made and smell their stench drifting through the air. They stank of rotten things: sewers and rancid meat.

'Do people still use this bridge?' I asked as we approached it. 'Because I have an idea.'

'I'm open to all ideas at this point,' Vincent said.

I stepped on to the bridge, praying it wouldn't collapse, and felt the ropes swing. Below me was a deep, dry ravine that dropped about thirty metres, and must once have been a river – it cut through the ground, long and wide, splitting the land in two. I smiled.

'Let's get across, then cut the ropes,' I said. 'Some creepers will be forced back, the rest will fall in. I don't think they'd chase us after that.'

'What?!' Vincent looked amazed, and then his expression shifted – suddenly he looked like Christmas had come early. He knew now we stood a chance of escaping from the creepers' pursuit in one piece.

I signalled that, once we were over the bridge, he should use his sword to cut the first set of ropes and I would do the same to the second.

'Do you think this is going to work?' Vincent asked.

'I hope so, because if it doesn't . . . Well, I'll see you in the afterlife.'

We tried to cross the bridge as fast as we could, but its wooden planks were old and rotten, so we had to keep looking down and treading carefully, taking it one calculated step at a time, even when we could feel that the first creeper had stepped on to the bridge behind us, gaining ground. I could hear some of them blowing up, a sure sign that they were all primed to attack the only prey in sight – the two of us.

'I really hope one of them doesn't blow up the bridge,' I said.

'I hope so too,' Vincent replied. 'Although they're not clever enough to do that on purpose. That's the best thing about creepers – they're stupid.'

'You talk like you've come across them a lot.'

'More times than I would have liked,' Vincent said.

I sped up; I couldn't be as careful as I wanted to be, but I tried as best as I could not to put my feet through any holes. It was hard holding on to the rope with one hand and carrying the sword with the other. I was nearly at the other end of the bridge by now; there was a tower in the distance, rising high against a sky that already showed signs of nightfall approaching. Hopefully that tower was part of the temple we were searching for.

'You cut off the left side!' I said, running towards the ropes on the right. 'I really hope this works . . .'

Determined to do whatever it took to save our lives, Vincent and I began severing the ropes, but then I realized they were made of thick strands of cobweb and were hard to cut. I landed blow after blow on the rope as the creepers crossed the bridge in a line. The first one fixed his eyes on me.

A few more blows from the sword and at last the rope began to fray.

I looked back up at the creeper leading the pack; he was running fiercely towards me, just a few metres away now.

Four metres.

Three metres.

The stench of rotten meat was unbearable, but I carried on striking blow after blow, harder and harder. I had nearly done it – just a few more blows from my sword would make the difference between life and death.

'Cut it!' shouted Vincent, who had just that second managed to sever his own rope.

'I don't know if you've noticed, but I'm trying, you idiot!' I yelled back.

I struck the rope.

One blow.

Two blows.

Three blows.

Then I heard the noise of a burning fuse, the unmistakable sign that a creeper was about to explode . . .

I raised the sword as high as I could. My heart was beating fast, pounding in my chest. Dread ran cold through my veins as the first creeper closed the remaining space between us. Then I closed my eyes and brought the sword down hard for the last time. I felt the heat from a creeper explosion hit my face, I smelled burned hair, and I hoped there was a life after death.

CHAPTER 8

THE BRIDGE FALLS

The massive blast flung me on to the ground. It was followed by a sudden glow and a wave of unbearable heat but my strategy had worked – at the very last possible moment. The bridge had collapsed, sending most of the creepers tumbling to the bottom of the ravine. The first one had exploded in an attempt to blow us up, but he was already falling by then, so all he'd managed to do was burn my face and scorch my hair a bit. Now the bridge was gone, there was no way anyone could cross the ravine unless they made a detour of several kilometres – much to my relief.

As creepers are complete idiots, those left on the other side still walked right up to the far edge of the ravine and carried on, apparently not realizing there was no longer a bridge for them to step on to. One by one they hurtled into the ravine, plummeting right to the bottom of the dried-out riverbed. Their explosions made the pit deeper and caused landslides as they fell, burying other creepers beneath them. I didn't feel the slightest bit bad about that.

'I guess we did it,' I said. 'God, I can hardly feel my feet. I wish I hadn't skipped P.E. so often.'

Vincent bent forward, his hands on his knees. 'Me too,' he said. 'But we have to press on – it'll be nightfall soon and the monsters will be coming out.'

'To the temple?'

'That's right.'

I stared at the temple. I could see it more clearly now. It had towers and a vaulted roof; although the whole place was now in ruins, I could tell it must have been really beautiful once. I wondered how much of its damage had been down to the passage of time and how much was down to Herobrine and his army.

'My last hope of defeating Herobrine is here,' said Vincent. 'A very powerful priestess used to live here, and she was the only person alive who knew all the legends and prophecies surrounding Herobrine. I'm hoping she's left something useful behind.'

We plodded along slowly; neither of us could walk fast after what we'd just been through.

'What if we don't find anything?' I asked.

'We adopt Plan B,' Vincent said. 'We try to gather people together and fight against Herobrine, one army against another.' His tone wasn't optimistic about the outcome of such a battle.

'I hope it doesn't come to that,' I said. 'All I want is to get back home and never play Minecraft again. After everything I'm going through here, I solemnly swear I will only play *League of Legends* and *DotA*.'

Vincent smiled. 'No one plays *DotA*.'

'I do,' I replied, pretending to be insulted. 'I still play *Ragnarok Online*. I'm *old school*.'

We were already close to the temple, so I could see it properly now. Some of its walls had collapsed; there was evidence of fire and holes caused by creeper explosions, but still the temple's architectural structure looked pretty amazing, and I was awestruck by the size of it. There was a sign in a corner.

THE PRIESTESS'S TEMPLE

I CAN READ YOUR FORTUNE. I CAN BRING

YOUR MISSING HUSBAND OR WIFE

BACK TO YOU IN THREE DAYS.

SPECIAL OFFER: BUY TEN CONSULTATIONS,

GET THE NEXT ONE FREE!

I smiled after reading that – someone had a good sense of humour. In the past, hundreds of people must have come here and felt awed by this place. It was sad to see it now, all in ruins and falling apart.

Vincent signalled that we should go inside. I led the way, walking up the steps towards huge double doors made of gold. As we walked our footsteps echoed, ringing out like struck metal on the temple floor. Everything was silent; as night fell around us, the sound of our own footsteps was almost frightening.

'Be wary,' murmured Vincent.

'I'm always wary,' I told him.

I lifted my sword in readiness, and Vincent did the same. We were ready to strike back if any creature crossed our path. This time of day, when the sun was disappearing, was the worst of all – you never knew when or where danger might appear. Pacing through the temple, we turned left and reached a hall.

'I think we're alone here,' I said. 'We should find a place to set up camp. All we need to do is to light some torches – the monsters won't come near us if we create enough light.'

'That's a good plan,' Vincent said. 'We're not going to be able to find anything useful in this temple in the dead of night.'

But, yet again, Murphy's law proved itself to be true – the universe always conspires for everything possible to go wrong.

When I turned into the hall, distracted, with my sword down, I bumped into something. Something slimy that smelled of gunpowder and rotten meat.

Something that was making a sound like a burning fuse.

CHAPTER 9

A CHASE IN THE DARK NIGHT

For Notch's sake! I thought as I looked down and saw a creeper right in front of me. It froze when it saw me. I could just hear the burning-fuse noise; all I could think was that it was about to blow up.

The creeper stood perfectly still. I was scared to death, too panicked to even take advantage of those few seconds to run away. Instead I raised my arms to protect my face from the blast, but . . . nothing happened.

'Wait, what . . . ?' I trailed off.

The creeper just turned round and ran in the opposite direction, its four legs pounding on the floor, the burning-fuse noise still hissing through the air.

'He must be going to get reinforcements,' said Vincent. 'We have to kill him before he reaches them.'

Getting rid of one creeper is easy when you're playing Minecraft on the computer. All you need to do is to get close to it, strike it, and then run away before it blows up. But Vincent was right: if this creeper was about to summon a horde as big as the one that had just chased us, we'd be done for. We were exhausted and ill equipped; we'd never survive.

'OK,' I said, breaking into a run. I was still terrified, but finally my survival instinct had kicked in.

So we chased after the creeper as best we could. We were so exhausted, hungry and thirsty that every step we took felt like a challenge. We followed the creature's footsteps as it zigzagged away from us; it seemed to know this place like the back of its hand, squeezing through shortcuts as it raced along the halls. I held my sword tight as I pursued the creeper, sweat running down my face, my whole body aching.

'It's going to sneak into that tunnel!' shouted Vincent.

I looked to where Vincent was pointing and saw a hole in the hall's right-hand corner. The creeper slipped into this dark exit hurriedly and disappeared from view. Its friends must have been at the end of that tunnel.

'I think we should go back,' I said. 'The creeper's already too far away – we won't be able to catch it. We'd better just get out of this temple before another whole horde of creepers comes out.'

But Vincent just ran even faster, pushing himself to the limit. 'I haven't come all this way to give up now,' he called. 'I'm sure the answers we're looking for are in this temple. They *must* be here.'

He reached the hole and crept into it. I followed him. Inside, a long, steep path led down sharply away from us and into the gloom; we walked on top of rubble, stone blocks, piles of broken objects, old clothes and pebbles. We clambered over all of these obstacles as fast as we could, with me collecting a few more scratches on the way. Neither of us spoke; we just plodded on through that long, dark tunnel, waiting for a new pack of monsters to loom out of the darkness and kill us both.

'I can hear that creeper,' said Vincent. 'We'll catch up with it in no time. Keep up with me, and prepare yourself for battle.'

I took a deep breath and walked on. Up ahead there was light – to my surprise I spotted a torch on the wall. Its light revealed the creeper and a red door at the end of the tunnel. This torch was the only source of light we'd come across since we'd stepped into that place. Just as Vincent drew close enough to strike the creeper with one heavy blow, it opened the door and slipped through.

'Hang on,' I shouted to Vincent. 'Don't go in there!'

Vincent ignored what I'd said. He just ran through the doorway with his sword in his hand and a furious expression on his face.

All I heard then was a cry of pain.

And it wasn't from the creeper.

CHAPTER 10

MR LETTUCE AND HIS FRIENDS

I didn't hesitate for so much as an instant. As soon as I heard that cry of pain I shoved my way through the door, wielding the sword in my hand and screaming, ready to attack the creeper with all my strength. Vincent was my only companion in this world – I wasn't going to let some stupid green monster finish him off.

The moment I stepped through the door I was flung forward and landed headlong on the floor, my sword skittering out of my reach. This was it, then. I felt sure I would be dead in an instant . . . but I was so tired of everything that I almost didn't care.

'All right, creeper,' I said. 'You can blow up. Do what you do.'

The answer was swift. But it wasn't exactly what I expected. I had braced myself for a surge of heat and a loud blast, but all I heard was a calm, female voice.

'And why would he do something like that? Mr Lettuce knows better than that, my dear. He's the best butler in the Overworld.'

I looked up and found myself surrounded by blocky-looking people – mobs, and a huge variety of them, too. There were some Steves, a few villagers with a cow, and, directly in front of me, a golden-haired female mob wearing a long white dress. On the other side of her, Vincent was sitting on the floor. His hands had been tied together by an old man who had a long grey beard and was dressed in black. This old man looked like the kind of guy who didn't have many friends.

'Who are you?' I asked, trying to stand up.

The woman stretched out her hand to help me. 'My name is Alex,' she said. 'I'm the priestess of this temple. I was the one who gathered all the villagers here, and together we built this underground city to help us hide away from Herobrine.'

I looked around; all eyes were set on us. There

must have been about forty people around us. There were several tents that looked like they served as people's homes, and many brightly lit tunnels stretched away from us on all sides of the cavern. The creeper we had been chasing stood by the priestess's side, keeping its eyes on me.

'Everyone gets scared when they meet Mr Lettuce for the first time,' said the priestess. 'Creepers have a bad reputation around here. The same thing happened with the Users who came before you – they were scared to death.'

'What happened to them?' I asked.

Alex remained silent.

'Hasn't your friend told you what happened to the Users?' asked the old man dressed in black, the one who looked like a sort of ninja. His hand rested on the sword by his waist, and his voice was firm. 'Hasn't he told you what he did? How Noobie Saibot and Punk-Princess166 were driven out of this world because of him?'

'Don't believe anything he's saying, Bia!' shouted Vincent. 'He's just an old man, he doesn't know anything – don't believe what he's saying!'

The old man slapped Vincent across the face and then walked over to me. There was some sort of confusion, muffled talking and swearing around me – something was happening, but I didn't have the slightest idea what it was. I tried to move towards Vincent, but two angry-looking men with big noses blocked my way. They stood in front of me while the old man walked towards the centre of the space, and a crowd of mobs gathered around him.

'Ladies and gentlemen, boys and girls,' he said. 'May I have the pleasure – or rather, the displeasure – of introducing you to the person who's to blame for everything, the one who tried to enslave us all in his castle in City 01. The one who set Herobrine free. Here he is, the Overworld's enemy . . . the Red King.'

I couldn't believe my ears. I turned towards Vincent. It didn't seem possible that the kid who had saved me from an enderman, who had run beside me as a horde of creepers pursued us, was the biggest griefer on Earth. Someone who destroyed other people's games just to get a kick out of it. In fact, he had even done it to me – one day I had turned on my computer to discover that a so-called Red King had wrecked a house I'd spent months building.

'Bia!' Vincent shouted. 'You have to let me explain. You need to let me speak, please – things have changed.'

I couldn't take any more. I was filled with rage, and all of it was directed at this person, the person behind everything – the person who had set Herobrine free.

GRIEFERS

By Punk-Princess166

Griefers are horrible people who like to destroy biomes and other people's constructions, and who also probably aren't even capable of tidying their own bedrooms.

It's best to keep well clear of them. They can do away with hours and days of hard work, destroying landscapes you've created, and even wrecking entire worlds.

Griefers seem to do it all just for the sake of being hated, as though being known as a griefer is actually a good thing.

As well as physically destroying things, griefers can be bullies too. They insult and upset people, swearing and teasing. Basically, they are a real pain.

Don't feed the monster.

Never let a griefer get away.

CHAPTER 11

THE RED KING

I stared at Vincent. I still couldn't believe that the person I had been travelling with was the worst person in the whole of the Overworld. There are billions of people in the real world – but there I was, spending my time with public enemy number one.

The old man in black approached me and put his hand on my shoulder.

'I see you've been fooled by the Red King too,' he said. 'Everyone in the Overworld knows how dangerous this scoundrel is. My name is Hattori Hanzō. I am the last samurai and I fought against Herobrine with the Users who came before you.'

Vincent tried to stand up, but one of the villagers

hit him hard on his back, holding him down so he couldn't move. They had him under control.

'You have to listen to me,' Vincent said. 'Things have changed. I'm trying to defeat Herobrine. I'm not the same person I was before.'

'Defeat Herobrine?' the samurai repeated. 'You were the one who set that creature free from the Nether! You and your greed were what released him from his prison, and caused all the destruction that followed.' Then Hattori Hanzō signalled to the villagers, and they began to drag Vincent away.

I stayed there, motionless. There was nothing I could do or say. I'd travelled with Vincent all this time, and if I hadn't come across these people, he would still have been my first and only friend in this world – the person who had saved me from an enderman and run with me as the creepers chased us. Finding out that he was the Red King . . . It was a huge shock. But part of me wanted to believe people can change – that you should always be given a chance to put right any mistakes you might have made in the past.

'Come over here, Bia,' said Alex the priestess.

'Hattori and I have a lot to talk to you about. You're a User – you could be exactly what we need in our fight against Herobrine.'

I didn't reply. As I walked beside the two of them I felt a sort of emptiness, as though I had betrayed Vincent. I couldn't help but think that these people could be lying – why should I trust this bunch of pixelated square-shaped people more than someone who had already gone through so much by my side?

We carried on walking through the cavern; several pairs of eyes watched me curiously, tracking every step I took. They had built a magnificent hiding place down here – it had tents, tunnels and secret entrances. I could hear the sound of running water too, which meant there was a river near by, so nobody needed to venture out from their subterranean world to get water.

Alex, her butler – the creeper – and the samurai led the way, walking towards a large red tent that was pitched in one of the corners of the cavern. Dark smoke billowed through a hole in its roof.

'I think she's creating something,' said Alex.

Hattori Hanzō smiled. 'She's always creating

something. I don't think she's ever got over losing that balloon. I bet she'll be delighted to find out who we have locked up now.'

I didn't feel like talking, so I just stood there in silence. All I wanted was to get back home as fast as I could. I missed my mum, my dad, and even our silly cat that was always shedding tufts of hair all over my bed. I missed everything – everything except this world of blocks and pixels.

'Amelia!' called the samurai. 'You have some visitors.'

I wiped away the tears running down my face and tried to be strong as we walked into the red tent. There was so much smoke inside that it was hard to see. Tools, spare parts and dirty plates lay all over the place, and everything was covered in grease stains.

I heard swearing and the sound of things being knocked over, then a figure appeared through the smoke. She was dark-skinned like me, and was wearing a leather jacket and aviator goggles. She was covered in soot and held a wrench in her right hand.

'Punk-Princess166? Is that you?' she asked. But, as soon as she could see me more clearly, she looked disappointed. 'Ah. I thought you were someone I knew.'

Alex stepped forward and smiled at the woman in the leather jacket. 'We'll see them again, Amelia,' said the priestess. 'We've got a new chance to fight against our enemy. A new User is here now, and she may just be our miracle.'

I couldn't help wondering what those previous Users had been like – everyone seemed to hold them in such high esteem! Perhaps they had been gifted or even geniuses. Maybe they were like my neighbours, Arthur and Mallu, or maybe they were more like Einsteins. And if even they hadn't managed to succeed when they fought against Herobrine, what chance did I stand? I was just a dull, ordinary girl from a dull, ordinary place.

'You haven't told her the best part, Alex,' Hattori Hanzō said. 'We've just captured a very important prisoner. We've finally caught the Red King.'

The woman's eyes lit up so brightly it was as if a thousand lamps had been turned on inside her head.

She tapped the wrench against the palm of her hand. 'Take me to that idiot,' she said. 'It's about time he paid for the balloon he destroyed.'

Alex smiled. 'There will be time to settle that debt, but right now we need to discuss something rather more urgent,' she said. 'We have to talk about how we can make sure Herobrine doesn't find the ender dragon.'

THE END

By Punk-Princess166

There are legends about a place beyond the Nether and the Overworld. It's in this legendary place that the ender dragon supposedly lives. The place is called the End, and it is the end of everything, a place where they say nothing can be created. It is said to be like a void, and it's the place where endermen come from.

I really hope this place doesn't exist, because if it does, it means the dragon is real too.

And if the dragon is real . . .

Then I hope you're ready for your funeral.

CHAPTER 12

THE ENDER DRAGON

No one spoke for quite some time. Hattori stared at the priestess with a worried expression; Amelia looked as though she had been hit in the stomach, and I just stared at them all since I had no idea what was happening. Which had kind of become the norm ever since I set foot in this place.

'How do you know that?' asked Amelia. 'The ender dragon is just a legend.'

The priestess shook her head slowly from side to side. 'I had a vision,' she said. 'I saw Herobrine, as clearly as if he was next to me. He was talking to an old man in a library – he wanted to find out how he could set the ender dragon free. The librarian refused to give him any information, and so Herobrine killed him.'

There was silence. They all seemed terrified by what they'd just heard.

'Are you sure this is true?' asked Hattori Hanzō. 'You've often said that your visions don't always come to pass.'

The priestess nodded firmly. 'I'm sure about what I saw,' she responded. 'It wasn't a premonition of the future, it was a vision of something that was actually happening in that moment.'

'What are we going to do now?' I asked. 'If Herobrine manages to set the dragon free, we're in real trouble. Maybe we should ask Vincent what he knows about this – I've known him for a little while now, and he is determined to fight against Herobrine.'

Hattori Hanzō laughed loudly. 'I don't doubt that he is,' he said. 'The Red King set Herobrine free hoping he would be able to control him and conquer the Overworld, but he ended up being beaten. I'm sure he's keen on taking revenge. But I for one will not forget who he really is and what he did to this world.'

I stepped forward. There was no doubt that we should challenge the way Vincent had behaved, but we were at war – we had to do whatever it took to deal with our enemy. Whatever price we had to pay would be nothing compared to saving two worlds.

'Vincent was a griefer, I'm well aware of that,' I said. 'He destroyed a construction of mine that I'd spent months building. But for God's sake, the situation we face is different now. If Herobrine manages to reach the edge – the boundary between the Overworld and the real world – then both worlds will be wiped out. You don't need to like Vincent or to trust him, but right now you're not in a position to turn away anyone who might be able to help.'

The mobs said nothing – they just stared at one another with their heads down. I couldn't pretend to know what they had gone through, what they had lost. Until I arrived in the Overworld I hadn't even thought that there could be intelligent life inside my computer. But I did know what happened when people didn't put their differences aside and work together: they all lost, and they all died.

At last, after a minute had passed, Alex patted my shoulder. 'The User is right,' she said in a calm voice. 'We need all the help we can get, even if that means siding with old enemies.'

Amelia just shrugged her shoulders. 'I don't mind having a chat with him,' she said, 'as long as I can punch him in the face when this is all over. Anything that will help us remove Herobrine from our world is a good thing.'

'I can't say that I like this idea,' the samurai told them. 'But I know that there are times when the priorities of war take precedence over personal views.'

I nodded and smiled. Despite what Vincent had done in the past, I wanted to believe that people could change, and that he was really on our side, fighting against Herobrine. If we gave up on that belief – on the idea that people could change . . . then it would be better if all worlds were destroyed altogether.

'Trust me,' I said. 'He's changed. He's on our side now. All we need to do is to talk to him and ask him for help.'

Hattori Hanzō crossed his arms. 'The Red King has already proved himself to be a person who has no honour or courage, and nothing can change that. But I trust your word, as I trusted the word of your predecessors, so we'll do whatever you think is best, User.'

The samurai conveyed no emotion as he spoke, and, when he'd finished, he just turned and walked away. I'd got what I wanted, but there was a sour taste in my mouth, as if I'd bitten into a lemon with its rind still on. The rest of the group left but I stayed where I was, and the tiredness from the past two days suddenly took over.

CHAPTER 13

TALKS IN THE TENT

Hattori, Amelia and Alex were halfway across the camp by the time I caught up with them. They were heading for the place where Vincent was being kept as a 'guest'. I truly hoped things would work out and we could all do this together. I knew Vincent wasn't exactly the most popular person in this place, and I was worried he would be attacked by someone. That was what I'd felt when I'd seen the way all the mobs sheltering here had stared at him – and at me, the User who had accompanied the Red King who had destroyed their homes and their lives.

'The Red King is in that tent,' Alex said, pointing out a yellow tent guarded by four men. 'We had to take measures in order to protect both the citizens and the prisoner. That's why there are guards and why he is being kept isolated.'

I nodded. I had already assumed that they would have taken all sorts of precautions to make sure that their most important prisoner couldn't escape. On the way to the yellow tent we bumped into Mr Lettuce, who had brought us each a slice of cake and a hot cup of tea. I was so hungry I grabbed them off him as we walked by.

I followed Alex, Amelia and Hattori Hanzō into the tent. It was very dark inside; the only light came from one torch that had been left there to keep monsters away. It was stiflingly hot, so much so that I began sweating right away, the droplets running down my neck.

'Hello, Red King,' said the samurai. 'We've got some questions we hope you can answer.'

Vincent was sitting on the floor with his hands tied to a wooden post behind his back. His hair fell over his face and all his protective armour had been removed. When he heard the old man's words, he smiled and looked up at us. 'You may not know, but

I stopped being the Red King a long time ago,' he said. 'So you can call me Vincent.'

The samurai remained impassive. 'We haven't got time for foolish jokes,' he said, his voice serious and firm. 'In my view, you should have been executed, but the User has pleaded for you, and has said that you may have some information that would be useful to us.'

Vincent stared at me, and I realized he was angry with me – perhaps because I had abandoned him and hadn't been imprisoned alongside him.

I smiled at him and tried to speak with a firm voice, but that was never going to happen. 'Hey, Vincent,' I said. My attempt at casualness ended up sounding more like despair. 'I told them you're a good guy, and that things have changed. They need your help. *I* need your help.'

He burst out laughing. 'They need my help?' he repeated. 'What a pity, Bia. It seems they've tied up the only person who can help them.'

Amelia stepped forward and clapped her hands as though she was applauding at the end of a play. Then she looked straight at Vincent and smiled. 'A brilliant performance, young man,' she said. 'But please. You must have known we'd react like this. Or did you expect to be welcomed by everyone here with open arms? You were the one who set Herobrine free, tried to enslave us, and stole all the redstone to build City 01. And it seems you're still the same spoiled brat you've always been.'

Vincent hung his head in silence, swallowing hard before replying. His answer came slowly, and he choked up as if he was about to cry. 'I know everything I did was wrong – every last bit of it,' he said. 'But things have changed. *I* have changed. I've done wrong, and I can't change the past, but I can do something now to pay for my sins. Go ahead and kill me . . . but I'm the only person who can help you defeat Herobrine.'

I couldn't think of what to say, so I stood still and stayed quiet. I didn't know whether I could ever really trust Vincent again, although it was true that I'd seen him trying to improve things. My mother had always told me that people needed forgiveness, that everyone deserved a second chance to put things right. And I strongly believed that no one should be punished forever for something they had done in the past. So I mustered some courage and finally spoke.

'I believe in you, Vincent. You've been an idiot, but I believe what you're saying.'

'Pity that doesn't help with the tying-up,' Vincent replied. 'But thanks for the moral support. It's better than nothing.'

Alex stepped forward. The priestess walked slowly with her dress sweeping along the floor as she approached the prisoner. She kneeled before him and looked him in the eye.

'The Overworld's destiny and your own world's destiny are both in your hands,' she said. 'You can either join us and help us or wait and be killed when we're attacked by our enemy. If you really want to show you've changed, then tell us everything we need to know about Herobrine.'

Vincent shrugged his shoulders. 'What would you like to know?' he asked. 'How he's plotting to set the ender dragon free and ride it from one world to another, breathing fire all around him? Maybe I know that. Maybe I also know where you can find the librarian who keeps Herobrine's prophecy and knows how to interpret it.'

Hattori Hanzō shook his head with a disappointed expression on his old, wizened face.

'We've already heard about the ender dragon,' said the samurai. 'And we've heard about the librarian too. He's dead now. Herobrine killed him.'

Vincent grinned. 'I thought he would,' he said. I heard something like pride in his voice. 'I suspected this would happen, so I sent the real librarian to a far-off biome, leaving someone else in his place at the South Temple. No wonder I became the Red King – I really am smart.'

Beside me, Amelia laughed out loud. 'What a pity you couldn't foresee that Herobrine was going to kick your butt,' she said. 'And that he'd destroy everything you'd conquered. Not that I minded the part when he kicked your butt, of course.'

Vincent ignored her and looked at Alex. 'Do you really want me to tell you everything I know?' he asked. 'All right. But grab a chair – there's a lot I have to talk to you about.'

CHAPTER 14

DOUBTS

All of us — except Vincent — left the tent that was being used as a prison. Then we gathered in Alex's tent, which was much bigger and had all sorts of statues, scrolls of paper and cushions scattered around it. I dropped on to one of the cushions and waited as the others sat down and made themselves at home around me.

Vincent's words were still buzzing in my head. I couldn't stop thinking about everything he had told us, from the place where the librarian was in hiding to the way in which the ender dragon would be set free. Vincent had said that he knew about the ender dragon because he had already thought about taming it himself while he'd been the Red King.

I was always going to vouch for Vincent, but thinking about that . . . It sent a shiver down my spine.

'We can't trust him,' said Hattori Hanzō. 'We might end up being double-crossed and killed.'

'I don't think so,' I replied. 'Since I arrived here, he's saved my life twice. I don't think he wants to hurt me. I truly believe Vincent has changed. He could have attacked you earlier – he could have harmed you – but he didn't.'

Amelia stood up and paced back and forth. 'Maybe he really does want to help us defeat Herobrine,' she said. 'But how can we be sure this isn't just a plan to have his greatest enemy defeated so he can get back to the throne in City 01?'

I scratched my head. That was undoubtedly a possibility, but I preferred to think otherwise. If Vincent had really wanted to rule from his throne in City 01 again, he would have gathered all sorts of creatures, set up an army and coordinated a huge battle where many would have been killed. But he had chosen to do it all by himself – he'd opted to try and gather information by living in hidden bases, as though he'd wanted to pass unnoticed. It was completely different from the way that the Red King had behaved in the past.

'I've got an answer,' I blurted out. 'A guarantee that Vincent won't go back to the throne once all this is over . . . if we're even still alive then, that is.'

All eyes turned to me, especially the samurai's – I knew he thought the only way out of this was to put Vincent in a dark corner with some zombies, or to lock him in a cage.

'Go on, girl, surprise me,' said Amelia. 'I think it'll be hard to convince us the old man's not got it right, but try your luck.'

I crossed my legs, settling down, and began explaining what I had in mind. It wasn't the best idea I'd ever had, but it would help get the mobs and Vincent to work together. 'It's this simple,' I said. 'Banishment. Once Herobrine is defeated, both Vincent and I will go back to the real world. We'll leave and we won't come here ever again. That way the two worlds are saved and City 01's throne remains empty.'

Alex stared at me and had a sip of the tea that her

butler had brought over for her to drink. Unlike the others, she was calm and showed no emotion. 'And how can we be sure that he will really do that?' she asked. 'Vincent has never given us any reason to trust him. Everyone here knows that I, more than anybody else, have the right to ask for him to be executed. However, I'm prepared to do a deal with him, as long as it means that the Overworld is saved.'

I stared back at the priestess, intrigued by what she had just said.

As if he sensed my confusion, Hattori Hanzō touched my arm and explained. 'Alex's mother was killed on the orders of the Red King. She was a fortune teller too, like Alex is now, and she predicted things about Herobrine that the Red King wanted to know.'

The news hit me like a punch in the stomach, and I had to try hard not to swear out loud. What really struck me was the calm way in which Alex seemed to be coping with all this. If I'd been in her place, I would have taken revenge the moment I set eyes on Vincent. I guess as a priestess she must have been taught to keep her emotions under control, even if deep down she was full of rage.

'I'm so sorry to hear that, Alex. I'm sorry about everything,' I said. 'It must be so hard for you. But I promise Vincent and I will leave the Overworld when this is finished. Getting back home to be with my family again . . . That's what I want most of all.'

Alex took a deep breath. 'Do you really trust him, User?' she asked. 'Do you really think that the person who killed my mother, and so many other mobs, will turn his back on everything and leave when the time comes? That he would never try to get his throne back?'

I nodded. 'I do,' I replied. 'I feel sure that Vincent is ready to turn his back on this world and leave. You have my word. I am going to have a discussion with him, and I am going to make sure this will all happen as I've said. You have my *word*.'

Everyone remained silent. Outside the tent, I could hear footsteps and muttered voices.

'You remind me of one of the Users who came before you,' said the priestess. 'She was just as stubborn as you are. Bia . . . if you really think that the Red King –' she paused – 'that Vincent has changed, then I'm prepared to believe you.'

I smiled. 'I really do think that he's changed,' I told her.

'Fine,' said Alex. 'Then let's do what Vincent has suggested. Hattori and Amelia, I hope you can get us prepared for this mission?'

The two mobs stood up and faced the priestess.

'We will do so, madam,' the samurai said. 'I'm going to get our weapons ready now; we'll set out at dawn.'

Just as they were leaving the tent, Amelia turned round. 'I'll make sure we've got all the food and equipment we need,' she said. 'On our last mission, Hattori took twenty swords, but not a single loaf of bread.'

They left then, and I was alone with the priestess. She seemed relieved for the first time.

'I'm counting on you to make sure Vincent honours our deal, and that, in doing so, he pays penance for all the pain he has caused me,' she said. 'If what the boy has told us about the library and the prophecy proves to be true, then this is our last chance to save both worlds and send Herobrine into the eternal sleep.'

'Leave it with me,' I said. 'He'll listen to me – I don't think Vincent is the same person he was before.'

Alex didn't reply; she just signalled for me to leave, so I left. I knew she had to work on some emergency plans and make sure everything was ready for tomorrow's mission.

Just for a second, on the way out, I thought I heard the priestess crying, but it could have been the wind blowing through the caves.

THE RED KING

By Punk-Princess166

Griefers are the worst kind of people. They destroy things just for the fun of it. They'll smash up everything in their way, and they'll do it on a whim. But, in all the years I've spent playing Minecraft and other games, I have never come across a creature quite like the Red King.

A self-centred boy with no love for anyone but himself. A kid who could have been a great player, taking advantage of the opportunities that Users have in the Overworld, but who instead chose to waste those opportunities by burning things down and destroying them.

I only saw him once, but I must say that, at the end of the day, I don't feel fear or anger towards him. I feel pity.

What could make someone's life go so wrong?

CHAPTER 15

A BIT OF A CHAT

While Amelia, Hattori and Alex were getting ready for the next day's journey, I headed over to the tent where Vincent was imprisoned. One of the guards tried to stop me, but in the end he stepped aside and let me in. Perhaps the fact that I had been released by his leaders at the very start helped to convince him.

I stepped into the tent and walked over to Vincent, who was still tied up and whose head hung down between his shoulders. He looked tired and uncomfortable. Before I sat down, he nodded at a jug of water and a glass. I poured some water into the glass and helped him drink it all; afterwards he immediately downed a second glassful.

'Customer care isn't so great here,' he said. 'This is the last time I'm staying here. I hope the manager is aware of the problem.'

Both of us laughed at that.

'I'll make sure the manager gets your feedback,' I said as I sat down in front of him and looked him in the eye. 'I've heard certain things about you here, Vincent. Things that you did – or rather, that the Red King did.'

Vincent shook his head slowly from side to side; his eyes drooped with tiredness and he sighed heavily. 'I'm the Red King,' he said. 'Speaking about him in third person won't change what I did. I lied; I destroyed places; I destroyed people. I'm not proud of it, but I can't deny it.'

'Alex said that you killed her mother, the woman who was the priestess before her. Apparently she knew certain things about Herobrine you wanted to find out?'

Vincent was speechless. Then I saw the corner of his mouth lift just a little, like an involuntary response that he couldn't control – like a goal kick that not even the fittest goalkeeper could save.

'Do you want to know the worst part?' he said. 'I don't remember any of it – not a trace of it. I know it's true, though. Back then I didn't care about people, I only cared about power. I'm so sorry for all of it. I'm really sorry.'

'It must be hard to deal with that,' I said eventually, in an attempt to break the silence. 'I mean it.'

'It's part of my punishment,' Vincent replied. 'I hope I haven't killed any of your relatives or destroyed your home.'

I burst out laughing. 'To tell you the truth,' I said, 'you did destroy one of my constructions. It had taken me months to build it, as well.'

Vincent smiled. 'I'm sorry about that,' he said. 'Next time I try to build an empire to rule for a thousand years, I'll be a lot more careful, I promise.'

I stared at the tent's yellow ceiling. Then I looked down and began doodling pictures in the dirt with my fingers, trying to imagine what having Vincent there must be like for Alex, and what it must be like for Vincent, having to deal with all the mistakes he had made, knowing that all of the Overworld tragedies, big or small, had his digital fingerprints all over them. Then I asked him a question that had troubled me ever since I had found out he was the Red King.

'Why did you do it?' I said. 'Everything you did when you tried to rule this place? You don't seem like a really bad person.'

'What do you know about really bad people?' he replied. 'There isn't a single wicked thing you can do in this world that I haven't done.'

'I trust you,' I said. 'I think something must have led you to do those things. A normal person doesn't just wake up one day and suddenly decide to become a tyrant . . . unless they're not well. That would be the only reason I could understand.'

Vincent smiled, shifting his legs and gesturing for more water. 'I don't know if I'm a normal person,' he said lightly, but I could tell he was just trying to hide how anxious he was. 'I was just like any other kid who plays day in day out without any friends – it was just me, my computer and my headphones. But sometimes other kids used to bully me at school. Every so often they would do stupid little things like hiding my belongings . . . but at other times I would get home from school with bruises. As time passed, I suppose I became more reclusive, delving deep into my games, venting all my anger on people, destroying the things other players had built. Becoming a griefer.'

I knew where the story was going. I had already witnessed other children going through the same on TV . . . and in my own family. People sometimes had to go through a lot just because they were different; there were people who kept it all inside, squeezed and crushed. As Vincent carried on talking, all I could do was listen in silence.

'I wanted to be far away from everyone who had hurt me,' he went on. 'And, one day, numbers began flashing in front of me on the screen as I played Minecraft and I ended up here. You couldn't get much further away than that – I was in a whole other world from the taunts and the people and the things that made me sad. Then it dawned on me that I could create a perfect place, so I made up my mind to save this world, even if doing so meant I had to destroy it first . . . I know that I was an idiot, but back then it all made sense.'

I smiled as supportively as I could. 'I guess when people are sad they do silly things,' I said. 'And I think that you've just proved me right. You aren't a bad person at all – just someone who got it wrong and is trying to fix it now. You should be proud of that.'

'Once all this is over, perhaps I will have something to be proud of,' he replied half-heartedly.

I rose and paced back and forth, wondering what to say next. In the end, I just said, 'I need to tell you something, Vincent. It's about your plan and what we're going to do if Herobrine is defeated.'

'What is it?'

'Alex wants to be sure that you won't betray us, and that if Herobrine is defeated, you'll go back to the real world with me. You have to leave this world in peace – and leave the throne behind you.'

Vincent sighed. 'I'd suspected they would make a request like this,' he said. 'I won't betray anyone, Bia, least of all you. I swear I'll leave this world when Herobrine has been defeated. Once that happens, my debt will be paid off. They'll never hear about me again.'

I agreed with him, and gave him a thumbs up as I began walking towards the exit of the tent. 'I think everything will be all right, Vincent,' I told him. 'Things will be different once you get back to the real world.'

'I hope so.'

I smiled. 'I know this isn't the comfiest place you've ever been, but you'd better take advantage of this time and get some rest. Go to sleep. Tomorrow is going to be a busy day.'

I turned and left the tent, ready to lie down and rest in the bed the mobs had prepared for me in a green tent in the corner of the cavern. There were butterflies in my stomach. I knew Herobrine had to be defeated. Only then could Vincent and I return home.

PART 2

THE HEROBRINE HUNTERS

CHAPTER 16

THE START OF ANOTHER JOURNEY

After sleeping on the hard mattress in the makeshift tent, I woke up with a pain in my back. Light shone through the green fabric walls, and outside I could hear the hustle and bustle of the villagers and other mobs who had been given shelter here after the devastation caused by Herobrine.

I put on my shoes and left the tent, feeling hungry. I wondered what had happened to Vincent after I'd last seen him. No one trusted him. Had he been given any food or anything more to drink?

People walked back and forth across the camp. Some were building weapons on crafting tables while others polished wood. There were some mobs preparing food in the furnaces, and, further down, a group was mining a wall, probably to make the place larger as well as to obtain ores. In the centre of the cavern, there was a big wooden table covered in plates containing different types of cakes, fruit tarts and omelettes, and bowls of steaming mushroom soup. My stomach rumbled; I was starving.

I grabbed a large empty plate for myself and put two generous slices of tart and two loaves of bread on it, and then I added some omelette on top of the bread. I carried it all as best I could, along with a jug of water and a wooden bowl full of soup. Then I sneaked into Vincent's tent. There were no guards at the tent's entrance today; perhaps I'd managed to choose the moment when they'd gone to the loo.

Vincent lay in a corner, and he turned when I entered the tent. His arms had been untied. He sat up on the floor, massaging his wrists, which looked sore from when he'd been tied up.

'Good morning,' I said.

'I'm glad someone is having a good morning,' he replied, smiling slightly. 'After spending a night here, I can say with confidence that this is the worst accommodation in the world.'

I smiled back and fetched a cushion to sit on, putting all the food and drink down carefully so that it didn't fall all over the floor. 'I thought you might be hungry,' I said. 'Who set you free?'

'The grumpy old man. In fact, he's just left.'

'Well, at least I wasn't caught plotting with the enemy,' I said.

He didn't smile this time; instead he looked a little sad. We ate greedily and I polished off half the soup in one go, wishing there was a soup as delicious as this in the real world, where mushrooms weren't half as tasty as they were here.

'I'm going to miss this food when we get back home,' I said, biting into a slice of pumpkin pie. 'I didn't even like pumpkin in the real world.'

Vincent ate some bread in silence; dark circles were visible under his eyes, as though he hadn't slept well the previous night.

'But I won't miss sleeping on the beds here,' I added, eyeing his tired face.

He smiled and shrugged his shoulders. 'I've never been a fan of soft beds, so this suits me fine.'

We finished eating and talked about nice things –

I thought he probably didn't want to dig into his past the way we had the night before. We talked about cartoons, anime and films, and shared adventure stories from the games we had played in the safety of our homes, on our computers, where everything was easy and where when you died all you had to do was press the RESTART key.

I didn't care about Vincent's past as the Red King. I was only interested in the kid in front of me who liked to talk about the same things as I did. I realized how alike we really were – just two ordinary teenagers who had ended up in the wrong part of the universe, brought together by a bizarre coincidence. After we finished talking we left the tent; Hattori was already with Amelia and Alex.

'Finally,' he exclaimed impatiently. He seemed a bit irritated. 'I thought you were still asleep.'

'I wouldn't have been able to carry on sleeping even if I'd wanted to,' I replied.

The samurai handed out some provisions and gave me an iron sword. He passed arrows and a bow to Alex and a sword to Amelia, who was packing her bag.

'Nothing for you,' said Hattori, looking at Vincent. 'I wouldn't trust you with a sword in your hands even if my life depended on it.'

Alex glanced sideways at Vincent, as if she felt a little disgusted in his presence. I threw a supportive look his way, and he drew his lips up slightly in a failed attempt at a smile.

'Are you coming with us?' I asked Alex.

The priestess smiled. 'I can't stay hidden here, safe underground, while my friends are risking their lives.'

'I hope I don't have to worry about you Users,' said Amelia. 'Now we are officially the Herobrine Hunters.'

I made a thumbs-up sign at that.

'Are we all ready?' asked the samurai, checking his supplies one final time.

We nodded. Vincent and I didn't have much to carry. The sword looked totally useless in my hands, especially as I was hopeless with weapons.

Hattori turned to Vincent, who opened his bag and removed the ender pearl, stretching his arm out and holding it in front of him. We gathered around him and put our hands on the pearl. Five people who could easily be walking into their own deaths, joined together.

'Herobrine is getting ever closer to setting the ender dragon free,' Alex said in a serious voice. 'This is our chance to win the war and rebuild the Overworld.'

And then everything vanished before my eyes.

CHAPTER 17

SPIDERS, CASTLES AND AN ABYSS

I felt as though my whole body had been drawn into my own navel. My hand burned as I held the ender pearl, and everything in my stomach stirred and rose to my throat. I took a deep breath, fighting the urge to be sick, and then suddenly everything went back to normal. The pearl was no longer there, and my body seemed fine; my nausea ended as quickly as it had begun. The darkness faded away and my feet felt as though they were standing on something soft.

I looked around. It looked like we had all gone through the same thing, except Vincent, who just stood there hanging his head in silence, staring blankly down at the ground.

Could people change? He was standing there by my side with his usual serious expression, clenching his fists. But I could see something frail about him, as if he was tired of everything that had happened, and was now on the verge of total exhaustion. I believed in him. People are complex – they're not just a sequence of numbers and pixels that will always lead to the same result.

We were on an island. There were green trees all around us, and the sea crashed against the rocks near by, bringing a rusty, salty smell with it.

Then I heard the sound of spiders' legs clicking all around us, between the shadows of the trees. Alex lifted her bow and Amelia and Hattori drew their swords, bracing themselves for the battle against the black, hairy tide of legs approaching, the hundreds of red eyes staring angrily out from between the trees. Spiders didn't usually attack during the day, but I quickly realized these were not ordinary spiders. They were much bigger than the ones I had come across in the game, for starters.

The three mobs didn't hesitate – they moved as though they were used to these sorts of battles, even the priestess, which surprised me. I, on the other hand, was holding a pathetic iron sword that I had no idea how to use. Vincent, who was by my side, only had his fists to fight with, as Hattori hadn't trusted him enough to give him a weapon. As I watched, Hattori knocked down three spiders, Alex shot arrows at some of the spiders that were further back, and Amelia screamed war-cries and laughed as she cut off spiders' legs. I tried to thrust my sword into Vincent's hands as one of the creatures approached us.

'No, hang on to it,' he said, putting his hand on mine; I closed my fingers tight around the cold metal of the sword's hilt. 'Do exactly what you would do in the game.'

I couldn't understand what he meant. Digital battles were completely different from real ones. In digital battles, all I needed to do to defeat my enemies was to press the keys over and over again. And if I died I would be born again, safely back at my spawn point.

I put those thoughts aside – there was no time to be distracted. A spider was almost on top of us, her front legs up in the air ready to attack Vincent, who was bracing himself to fight with his bare hands. As if by instinct, I held the sword tightly in my hand and ran towards the spider, striking her with all my might and without hesitation. I aimed for her front legs, cutting off her limbs with a sharp blow. The creature wailed in pain and crawled away, dragging the stumps of her legs. I jumped and dealt her a swift blow to the skull. She exploded in pixels that vanished into the air a moment later.

I stared at my own hands. I couldn't believe what I had just done. I looked up at Vincent and he smiled; just a slight smile on the corners of his lips, as if he knew what it was like to be astonished by your own unexpected act of bravery.

The three warriors kept on hacking away at the spiders, but it was as though a monster spawner was near by, causing more spiders to appear every second. Soon I began to think that we would be left with no other option but to run away.

'We have to get away from here!' Amelia shouted, just as I had the exact same thought. Her next words were lost under the sound of her sword striking a spider's body. All I heard was: '. . . to the castle!'

I looked further ahead and saw a black castle with a spire on the top of a large hill.

'Bia!' ordered Alex, drawing back her bowstring. 'Run ahead – we'll cover you.'

I nodded. I took one look at the path between the hills, trees and rocks ahead, and broke into a run. Vincent followed close behind me. A cluster of spiders tried to block our way, but I thrust at them with the sword, cutting off their legs, piercing their stomachs, stabbing their tiny red eyes.

Vincent called out and I saw that a clutch of spiders was approaching him. I threw my sword over to him and he caught it in the air, slaying spiders so fast my eyes couldn't follow his movements. He thanked me and we both ran on as fast as we could; Hattori, Amelia and Alex did the same behind us. The priestess kept shooting arrows to clear the way ahead as we ran through an area with dead mobs and pixels scattered all across the ground.

Running was a lot easier with my hands free, but

I didn't feel safe without the sword. I turned, stretching my arm out behind me and asking Vincent to give me my sword back, but with my next step I fell into a void.

Above me, Vincent flung the sword on to the ground and stretched out his arms to try and reach me, but I was already too far away. My body was falling fast – all the way down into an abyss. A chill grew in the pit of my stomach – a sign that the end was approaching. During those seconds I wished more than anything that I hadn't run without looking where I was going. Voices shouted my name. I felt the wind blowing through my hair, and watched the green world vanish before my eyes.

SPIDERS

By Punk-Princess166

Spiders usually won't hurt you during the day. It's as if the sun soothes them. But at night they will chase after you until they can pluck out a chunk of your leg, or even worse.

Fermented spider eye is great for potion-making. Cobweb can be used for lots of things too – it's as useful as string is in the real world.

Spiders don't pose a major danger to players; however, they *can* be dangerous when they attack in clusters.

CHAPTER 18

NUMBERS IN THE SKY

My elbow cracked and a throbbing pain shot down my arm. There was a deep gash in my right hand – the same hand that had caught hold of the sharp rock I was now clinging to. Below me there was a giant ravine; at its bottom I could just make out the glow of a pool of lava. I screamed, wedging my feet into the jagged cracks in the rock, trying to pull myself up and get out of the abyss. But the hand and arm that had stopped me falling were badly hurt.

With a huge effort, I looked up. I saw a mop of blond hair emerge over the edge of the stone cliff. Vincent was lying down on the ground above me and reaching his hand out towards me. His eyes were boggling with fear, just like mine. I stretched out my left hand to try to reach his fingers, but I couldn't. Then I began to feel my weakened right hand losing its grip on the stone. I felt sure that I only had a few seconds left. I tried to reach Vincent's hand again, but it was no use.

And then he was no longer there at all.

'Vincent!' I screamed. My voice was hoarse. A shudder ran through my body at the thought of falling fast to my death through these jutting rocks and into the pool of lava. I couldn't believe Vincent had just left me here – and to save his own life. The sound of battle could still be heard above so I assumed he'd taken advantage of the moment to run away – no one would have spotted him in the chaos. I shouted again, clinging to the rock with both hands and what little strength I had left. Just as I was about to let go, a thick white line slithered down the rocks until it touched my face. A cobweb string!

Vincent appeared again, lying at the edge of the ravine. I was overjoyed to see him – he hadn't abandoned me! He held the cobweb with one hand

and stretched the other down towards me.

'You're going to have to let go of that rock so that you can hold on to the string!' he called.

'I can't!' I shouted. My eyes filled with tears – maybe because of the wind, maybe out of fear. I knew that if I let go of the stone, I would be dead. But my right arm couldn't hold out any longer.

'You can do it, Bia!' shouted Vincent. 'Quick!'

Right above him, I could see spiders' legs stealthily appearing. There was no time to hesitate; there was no room for fear. I took a deep breath and let go with my left hand. Without thinking about what I was doing, just hoping that I would be fast enough, I reached out to grab the string of cobweb.

'Yes!' I whooped. I'd made it.

Vincent pulled the rope up until he could grab my hand and lift me back up on to the surface. I had no time to thank him – or to take a deep breath and feel the relief of having escaped death.

Because death was still there, right in front of my eyes. Without Vincent noticing, a spider had brought its sharp claws all but on top of him. I looked around quickly. My sword lay next to Vincent.

I rolled along the ground, grabbed my sword with my injured hand and stood up. I thrust the sword into the spider's thorax and it fell, dying at our feet. Vincent looked astonished as, with no strength left in me, I collapsed on to the ground.

There was another dead spider near by; the string of cobweb Vincent had used to save me was coming from its body.

'Just for a moment,' I said, out of breath, 'just for a moment, I thought you'd gone and left me.'

He smoothed his hair back from his sweaty forehead, dirtying his face with wet soil. 'Girl of little faith,' he said as he rose to help me up. 'I deserve a bit more credit than that.'

I laid one arm across his shoulders; the other hung hopelessly by my side, wounded, dirty and bloody. At least we'd got rid of the horde of spiders. Hattori, Amelia and Alex were fast approaching.

'Are you all right, User?' Alex said, slinging her bow over on to her back again and kneeling to look at my injured hand.

Amelia and Hattori's eyes were fixed on Vincent,

as though he was about to drop me into the abyss at the first opportunity.

'Hey, guys!' I said, a little irritated. 'Vincent helped me. If he'd wanted to hurt me, all he'd have had to do was let me fall into the abyss.'

Amelia and Hattori exchanged glances with one another, and Alex looked at me sideways. They didn't seem all that convinced, but I could understand why not.

'It isn't their fault,' said Vincent, helping me to sit down on the ground.

Alex began to examine my hand and arm closely.

'I wasn't the nicest person in the Overworld,' Vincent went on. 'I don't mind if you hate me. I just want to do what's right this time, and I hope I'm given the chance to do it.'

I reached to hold his hand in support, but he pulled away and walked off to sit down. I didn't try to imagine what was going through his mind, but it must have been hard, living with all that pain, and the weight on his conscience. I'd always had a comfortable life – aside from the school pranks, and the fact that I was always late – but what would

I have been like if I hadn't had a loving and supportive family?

A sudden pain in my hand snapped me back to reality. Alex was washing blood off my arm, and then she dressed the cut on my hand.

'What happened to you, Bia?' asked Amelia, staring at Vincent with distrustful eyes. 'Did the red kid do something to you?'

I shook my head. 'I fell into the ravine,' I told her. 'My hand was cut on a rock – I was trying to hold on to it.'

She seemed satisfied with the answer. Hattori finished off a spider that lay dying, and then returned to standing still again.

'How does the hand feel?' asked Alex when she was done. 'I just put some dressing on the wound, but hopefully it'll hold.'

I bent my arm and moved my fingers. 'It's still painful, but it's much better than it was,' I replied.

'You're a fast learner,' said Amelia, handing me back my sword after Alex had helped me up to my feet. 'I was impressed.'

'Honestly, I don't know how I did it,' I said. 'It

seemed like I'd done it loads of times, but I've never even held a sword in my hand before.'

'You have, clearly,' Hattori said. 'On the computer, on that thing you call a game. All the skills you learned there – whether it was using the keyboard or whatever else you had to do to play – that has become a real skill in the Overworld.'

'But at home it was just clicking on the keys,' I said, moving my fingers as if I was typing on a keyboard.

'It doesn't matter. There aren't any keys here, that's all,' Hattori said. 'Now we must continue onward.' He fixed his sword to his waistband and wiped the remnants of cobweb and spider blood from his arms. 'Let's go.'

Alex smiled at me, and I thanked her for dressing my injured hand. Amelia was still glaring at Vincent out of the corner of her eye as he stood up and headed towards the castle.

I left him alone and walked with the others. I held my sword in my left hand and played with it, realizing that I was getting used to it, as if it was something natural, something I carried every day.

Well . . . if Hattori was right, I *did* carry it every day. What else would I be able to do here, in this world of pixels and blocks?

We continued along the path, walking round the ravine I'd fallen into. A steep gravel road wound all the way up the hill, and as we journeyed on more and more trees dotted the countryside around us. We could see the castle clearly now, and it looked as though it had been built on top of a black rock. I wondered whether it was obsidian rock.

We eventually reached a giant staircase made from the same dark rock the castle stood upon. Hattori, Amelia and Alex began to climb the steps, leaving Vincent behind. I stood by his side as he stared up at the construction with his hands balled into fists, clenching his jaw.

'Did you build this?' I asked.

He nodded, then sighed as though he was disheartened.

'What's that rock? Obsidian rock?'

He glanced at me and then began to climb the steps. 'No,' he said, and then after a pause he added, 'It's bedrock.'

'*Bedrock?*' I asked, awestruck. 'But . . .'

'I could do anything I wanted in this world. Even modifications.' Vincent adopted a fake smile. 'But now I'm just a normal guy, trying to make up for all the mess I made.'

He looked up at the construction again with a sad expression. We were still only halfway up the staircase.

'I built this castle with bedrock so that it could never be destroyed, not even by the ender dragon. It's the perfect prison.'

As we walked further and further up the stairs, the sky grew darker. It was too early for night to be falling; I looked up, hoping to find that the sun had just passed behind a large cloud, but what I saw made my jaw drop.

'What is it?' asked Vincent, before looking up and seeing for himself.

The heavens turned black, and a sequence of ones and zeros spread across its surface, as though the sky itself was a giant screen whose light was dimming. Each and every single pixel in the air was now covered in numbers. They were the same numbers that had brought me here, flashing on and on before my eyes.

'What the hell is –' Amelia began as she stepped down to stand beside us, staring up at the sky and looking just as amazed as Vincent and I were. 'It can't be true.'

'What's happening?' It was Hattori's turn now.

Alex shook her head sadly. The numbers were reflected in her bright eyes. 'This is the end,' she said. 'I'm so sorry to have to tell you, Hattori, but that is what this is.'

Then, as if to prove the priestess right, the screen in the sky turned off . . .

And night-time took over the Overworld.

CHAPTER 19

LIGHT WAS GONE

'This is the end.' Alex repeated the sentence, stressing just how serious those words really were. 'Herobrine has won his greatest victory.'

It took a few seconds for everything to sink in and for me to realize what was actually happening.

It should have been daytime. Herobrine had destroyed the sun.

My heart pounded in my chest; my eyes struggled to make out the forms of my friends in the darkness. There was not a single source of light left anywhere. There wasn't even a star in the sky – the moon had disappeared. There was only darkness above. I realized then that Herobrine hadn't actually destroyed the sun. It was worse than that – he'd destroyed the entire sky, thus creating a permanent and everlasting night in the Overworld, the perfect universe for monsters to roam about freely.

'Daytime has been destroyed,' said Amelia. She sounded more angry than fearful. 'It's going to be night-time in the Overworld forever.'

Hattori brought us back to the here and now. 'We must get away from here as soon as we can,' he said.

We all understood his thinking and agreed with him. Soon there would be hostile mobs everywhere. As there was no light to deter the monsters, the whole of our journey was put into question, and until we found shelter our lives were at risk with every second that passed.

'We'll be safer inside the castle,' said Vincent.

Given that he'd built the place, I trusted him, so I strode up the steps behind him.

In no time at all the monsters began to emerge. I could hear their clicking, murmuring and wailing as they spawned all around us.

I couldn't fight with my injured arm, but still I held my sword tight.

Hattori drew one of his swords and discreetly handed it to Vincent. 'I hope I can trust you, Red King,' said the samurai.

'I am not the Red King any longer,' the boy replied. 'My name is Vincent.'

And then I walked straight into a skeleton that was sitting on top of a giant black spider. There were monsters everywhere!

Amelia moved to my side and, as soon as we'd seen off the spider-riding skeleton, we fought together against a gaggle of zombies. I wasn't able to strike the monsters particularly hard, but I was determined to carry on up the staircase, step by step, monster after monster, trusting that my companions would help me when I needed them.

Alex cleared the way, shooting arrows from her bow and always hitting the target.

Amelia moved away to kick a creeper until it fell down the staircase and blew up. Then she beheaded a skeleton trying to shoot her with an arrow. With every blow she let out a swear word. 'Can't. I. Have. A. Moment. Of. Peace?' she roared as she slew an enderman with a single blow of her sword.

I stayed by Vincent's side, and we climbed until
we reached a height where we could see two giant
doors. I stretched out my hand to use the door
knocker, but Vincent stopped me.

'No!' he shouted, as he bent down to pull his
sword from the chest of a zombie he'd just killed.
'It's a trap!'

I stepped back from the door as fast as I could,
but I was caught off guard – and punched hard in
the face by an enderman. It was about to strike
again with its long arms, but I managed to dodge it
quickly and slice it across the knees with my sword.

I heard Vincent scream behind me; I had just
enough time to see him clutching his thigh where an
arrow had buried itself in his flesh. Then the
enderman renewed its attack.

I struck at it again, but it disappeared and I
stumbled, unbalanced with no target to hit. Behind
me, I heard the sound the monster made as it
teleported back into place, and I thrust my sword
backwards. Success! I had struck it in the chest. The
enderman wailed as it moved away, leaving behind
a trail of purple smoke in the darkness.

I turned and saw Vincent staggering towards some kind of switch set into the wall on the left-hand side of the castle entrance. When he reached it, he pressed it hard, gripping on to the wall for balance. I guessed that back when he was the Red King he'd laid a trap to stop intruders, and now he needed to disable it so the door could be opened.

I darted over to him and helped him pull the door open as fast as possible so we could slip inside. Amelia, Hattori and Alex followed close behind us. We all leaned hard against the heavy doors, pushing them closed to hold back the monsters crowding around outside.

As soon as the door was fully shut, we stood in the pitch-black darkness.

The thick wooden doors and walls of rock muffled the sound so we could no longer hear the snarls and groans of the creatures outside; the only sound was our own heavy breathing, and the noise of an arrow being pulled from flesh, followed by a wail.

'Vincent!' I called out. I felt a hand holding on to my shoulder, as if he was trying hard not to fall.

No one else seemed to be concerned by his pain, but I couldn't see their faces, so I tried not to judge.

'Please, help me walk a bit further ahead, to the right,' Vincent said.

'I can't see anything.'

'I know, but there is nothing on the floor here,' he told me. 'You can walk safely.'

I moved slowly, afraid that I would bump into something or fall into a hole. But there was only a cold wall ahead of me.

Vincent let go of my shoulder and I heard him limp away, swearing in a low voice. Then there was the sound of a lever being pulled down, and suddenly the place was filled with light from several torches hung from the ceiling.

The glare hurt my eyes and I covered my face until my eyes adjusted, and then I looked around me.

The whole hall was made of black rock mottled with white, and it was decorated with paintings, bookshelves and chandeliers. There were two large lounges – one to the right and another to the left of us – and a white quartz crystal staircase lay ahead, with ornate columns on either side of it. At the top of the staircase stood two golden doors made of wood.

I was about to praise Vincent for his building skills but then I realized he was too distracted for that – he was sitting on the bottom step of the staircase, tearing his jeans around the place where the arrow had struck.

'Where's the librarian?' Hattori asked without hesitation.

I took no notice of the samurai. I ran to help my friend, who was now staring feverishly at the open wound on his white skin.

CHAPTER 20

A GLIMMER OF HOPE

I used my sword to cut a strip of cloth from my t-shirt, and tied the makeshift bandage round Vincent's leg to stop the flow of blood from his wound. I poured some water over the cloth and he groaned in pain. He looked pale.

'We haven't got time for this,' Amelia snapped. 'Where is the librarian?'

I snorted in irritation and tied another strip of cloth round the wound on Vincent's leg. I was glad that I was wearing a long t-shirt, given that I was having to tear off so much fabric – I would have been left with a crop-top otherwise. I helped Vincent up; he leaned against my shoulder and pointed to the top of the staircase.

'Up there, in the library,' he said, and we began to climb the stairs.

I stayed at Vincent's side and he leaned on me as we walked. I couldn't help but feel a bit upset by the way the others had ignored him, but I knew it must be hard for them to forgive him.

'Are there any other traps around here?' asked Alex, walking cautiously.

Vincent nodded. Sweat ran down his face, and his hair was sticking to his forehead; he wiped his fringe aside impatiently.

'Can you walk faster?' I murmured. I knew the others were in a hurry.

'I think so.'

We walked upstairs as quickly as we could and Hattori, who was ahead of us, opened the double doors. They led to a space that looked like a courtyard with an enormous garden. The courtyard was lit by lanterns and torches, and water cascaded from a fountain in the centre. Within the garden were pots of flowers and shrubs, as well as benches, all symmetrically placed round the fountain.

Vincent and I went ahead; he was walking more

steadily now. There was a door at the other end of the garden too. Before we walked through it, I heard Amelia let out a concerned sigh. When I turned, she was staring up at the sky, where there was nothing but endless blackness.

'Do you think we'll be able to sort this out?' she asked Alex. 'Or are we going to have to live in darkness forever?'

Her friend put a hand on her shoulder without looking up. 'Let's walk on and perhaps we'll find out,' she replied.

Hattori nodded his head in the direction of the door, and we walked towards it.

'In the Overworld, everything is possible,' said the samurai. 'The sky was created and then it was destroyed. Why could it not be rebuilt again?'

'True, but we have to defeat Herobrine before that can happen,' I said. 'And, just to remind you, he's the guy who destroyed daylight altogether.'

'We can't give up, Bia.' Amelia attempted a smile, but she didn't seem particularly hopeful either.

We walked through the door and turned to the right, into a poorly lit hall. Our footsteps echoed, and our voices sounded like screams in that silent place. We walked through another door that led to what looked like a reading room. Tables, chairs and red sofas were dotted around, and chandeliers formed of torches and lanterns hung from the ceiling, covered with sparkling gems.

We stood by the door, breathing heavily, unable to look away. Dead bodies lay everywhere – on the chairs, the tables and the sofas. It looked like the people here had been killed so quickly they hadn't even had time to defend themselves. Some lay face down on open books; others held pens or mugs full of drinks. One of them lay right in front of me, by my feet, his hand stretched out towards the door – perhaps in a failed attempt at an escape.

Hattori and Amelia swore in unison.

'What *happened*?' I asked.

Alex kneeled beside a monk copyist. 'He's still warm,' she said. 'We're just a moment too late.'

The glimmer of hope I had left was fading away. Herobrine had got there before us.

'We have to run.' Vincent let go of me and sprinted ahead as fast as he could with his injured leg.

We ran after him, heading up a short flight of stairs with bookshelves all around it, dodging the dead bodies as we went.

'How did he get in here?' asked Alex, on my tail.

'I have no idea,' replied Vincent, already out of breath, but still running. 'I swear I had nothing to do with this.'

'I knew we couldn't trust this brat!' Amelia growled.

'Enough of that, Amelia!' Alex snapped. 'We haven't got time for this. The boy has already shown us that he's trying to help.'

'And how do you explain this?' Amelia asked, pointing to a body of a man leaning against the wall as though he'd been killed while he ran. 'This castle is one of *his* hiding places.'

'Herobrine *turned off the sky*,' Vincent said. 'Finding my hiding place wouldn't exactly be too difficult for him.'

We ran through several hallways with bookshelves and piles of books on either side; it was like a labyrinth. We slowed down, following close behind Vincent. We turned left, then right, then right again, then left, and then left again, along what seemed to be a never-ending path. Then, finally, we got to its end.

'Stay there,' said Vincent, standing in front of a door. I saw him cut a string that was almost invisible to my eye. Another trap. 'The entrance's trap is untouched, so I think we made it in time.'

Hattori pushed him aside and stepped through the doorway. We went through right after him, our weapons in our hands, ready to deal with whatever we might find inside. The library occupied a massive space; it was three floors high and stacked with books. A chandelier hanging from the centre of the round ceiling lit the red carpet below, where there was an enchanting table with a closed book lying on its surface. There, right in front of it, stood a man whose presence filled us all with fear. His eyes glowed in my direction and I felt their gaze like a stab to my chest – as though that glow could hypnotize me, piercing through my skin and right into my heart. He was holding the Diamond Sword.

But its blade, instead of the turquoise colour I'd expected, was soaked in red.

The colour trailed off the blade, dripping into a fresh puddle on the floor beside a man who lay there.

We were too late.

HEROBRINE

By Punk-Princess166

I just need to say one thing: he is *bad news*.

CHAPTER 21

NETHER'S GHOST

We were speechless. I stood still, unable to look away from Herobrine's glowing eyes. For a few long seconds, it was as though my whole life had been suspended. I waited. I didn't know what to do.

Herobrine lifted his sword swiftly, wiping off the blood that was dripping from its blade and forming a trail on the ground. Had we got there a few minutes earlier – even just a few seconds earlier – everything might be different. But it was too late.

Beside me, Vincent clenched his fists, ready to attack our enemy. I jerked my head at him in warning and he stepped back. If we wanted to stand a chance against this creature, then we had to act with extreme caution. If even the previous Users,

Punk-Princess166 and Noobie Saibot, hadn't been able to defeat Herobrine, what was I going to manage to do?

Herobrine pushed the librarian aside with his foot; the body rolled over with a thud. Our enemy wasn't the slightest bit worried about us being here – we were like insects to him, and just as easily crushed. Herobrine smiled, his eyes shining in the gloom.

'You arrived at exactly the right time,' he said, then burst out laughing. 'I'm pleased to have you all gathered around for this moment. It's good to have people here to witness my victory.'

He stared at Vincent, a manic smile still visible on his lips as he spoke his next words. 'A child never stops being a child, as far as I know. Did you really think that I would work for a foolish boy like you?'

Vincent didn't speak, and I was pleased to see that he hadn't been caught up in Herobrine's childish teasing. Hattori, Amelia and Alex walked in front of Vincent and me until they were just a few steps away from Nether's ghost. The enemy looked at them scornfully.

'And what did you think of my masterpiece?'
Herobrine asked, stretching out his arms and looking
up towards a window, through which we should
have been able to see the stars and the moonlight,
but could only see darkness. 'The Overworld belongs
to me. It belongs to *me*, to the dead, and to all the
hostile mobs who roam this land. Pity you won't be
alive to see the same happen to the real world,'
he said.

'As if *that's* ever going to happen,' I said, mustering
my courage. 'Have you ever considered having your
own chat show? You're a natural-born comedian.'

Herobrine turned to me. He didn't look happy at
being interrupted in his moment of glorying in
his success.

Vincent moved closer to me. 'I brought you to
this world, Herobrine, and I can remove you from
it,' he declared.

And then, suddenly, everything happened at once.
In a flurry of noise, fury and confusion, all of us
charged at the same time, with a surge of attacks
and blows, sword against sword, arrows against
armour, blades against flesh and pixels. My sword

clashed against Herobrine's, but it had no impact. My attack was completely useless – Herobrine hardly even seemed to notice me when I charged at him. All my courage turned to dread. I looked around and saw that Vincent and the others were attacking, but every attempt failed as Herobrine shifted around easily and smoothly. Every blow against him was unsuccessful.

What kind of hope did we have against a monster like this?

Herobrine stepped away, unfazed. He seemed perfectly calm. No, more than that – he looked as if he was having fun.

'There is no hope for you,' he said. 'I took all the information I needed from the librarian.' He glanced down at the body lying on the floor. 'Soon I will set the ender dragon free, and the two worlds will be destroyed forever.'

'Stop showing off, you idiot,' growled Vincent, striking again. 'Hearing your voice really winds me up.'

Herobrine parried the blow easily and struck back, catching Vincent hard in the chest. Vincent flew across the library and landed in a heap on the floor at the far end of the room. He let out a wail of pain.

'Vincent!' I shouted.

Behind me our friends were fighting hard. The noise of screaming, swearing and the clash of metal on metal echoed around us, giving the impression that there were a thousand people fighting here instead of just four. My heart beat fast as I ran towards the boy collapsed on the floor, and I hoped against all hope that everything would turn out OK. But deep down I felt sure that it wouldn't. I kneeled by Vincent and helped him up. He shook his head and then pressed his hands to his forehead, as though he felt sick after the fall. His injured leg could barely take any weight now.

'You can't fight when you're like this,' I said. 'It's crazy.'

He snorted with anger, wiping his face impatiently. 'This is a nightmare!' he muttered, frustrated. 'We *have* to get rid of him.'

He tightened the strip of cloth around his wound and grabbed his sword from the floor.

'I have to defeat him,' he said, with his eyes fixed on the enemy, who stood just a few metres away. 'But how?'

Vincent wasn't paying any attention to me; he seemed to be lost in thought.

'Vincent!' I said, and he turned. 'What do we do now?'

He stared into my eyes, shaking his head a little from side to side. 'I haven't got the slightest idea,' he said. He looked deeply disappointed.

Like me, he had probably realized how useless our attacks against Herobrine really were. I bit my lip, unwilling to believe we had got so far and yet could do nothing. I thought about all the people in this digital world as well as all of those in the real world. I just could not accept that all of them would suffer because we couldn't work out how to fix this. After all, I must have fallen into this world for a reason. There are thousands of Minecraft players, and, out of all of them, *I* was the one who had ended up here. It couldn't just be a coincidence.

'According to the prophecy,' Vincent said, getting

his focus back, 'everything is linked to the Users and that sword.'

I looked towards Herobrine, who had levelled the Diamond Sword at Hattori's chest.

'But I don't know what to do,' Vincent went on. 'I had pinned my last hope on the librarian.'

I put my hand on his shoulder; I could see that this serious and stubborn boy was about to break, as though all the emotions he had so carefully concealed were emerging from him now as he crumbled. I barely had any hope left either, but I couldn't bear to let him give up. At least one of us had to stay strong, otherwise we'd end up feeding each other's despair.

I shook him gently.

'Vincent! We're going to make it! Are you listening?' I said. 'We're humans, and we created Minecraft! Isn't that what you said? That he's afraid of us?'

Vincent nodded, pressing his lips together, and then he turned towards the enemy of both our world and this one. 'Herobrine will fall,' he said, running to attack again.

I was right behind him. If my life was about to end, if there was nothing we could do, at least I would die fighting beside my friends. These people had not given up the fight after so many years; they had lost their families, their friends, their homes and their villages waging this war.

But, in the end, Vincent and I didn't even get the chance to rejoin the battle. It was over as fast as it had begun. I could hear Herobrine's loud laughter mingling with Alex and Amelia's screams. Screams that echoed through the library's bookshelves and between the books.

My eyes went wide and I let out a weak '*No!*', falling to my knees on the floor. Vincent stood where he was, his sword still lifted, his face contorted with rage. Amelia and Alex were standing in front of me, their eyes fixed on Herobrine's sword, which had stabbed Hattori Hanzō, running right through the samurai's body. The flush on his square face faded as he feebly gripped the blade.

Herobrine drew his sword back slowly and Hattori's body fell on to the floor. A brief murmur of pain escaped his lips. Then the enemy turned to us. His lips were shaped into a fine line across his face, and they twisted into a long wicked smile.

'There is no place left where you can hide,' he said. 'The world is night.'

CHAPTER 22

FAMOUS LAST WORDS

After those words, Herobrine just moved away from us – as if we weren't even worthy of his attention. His playtime was over, and now the children were left alone.

I couldn't move; I could only stare down at Hattori lying on the floor. Amelia and Alex ran up to him, and the priestess held the samurai's hand, lifting it to her tearful face.

'Hattori,' she murmured.

I noticed then that Hattori was still alive, clinging to the last remnants of his life. His chest moved up and down as he took his last gasps.

'It's going to be all right, old man,' Amelia said, pressing hard on the wound, trying to stop the blood. As it gushed out through the mercenary's fingers, she let out a little sob. 'Don't panic, OK? It'll be all right.'

Vincent was in front of me, motionless. His mouth was half open and his eyes were wide. He hung his head and dropped his sword; it clattered as it hit the cold floor, the only sound to be heard in the library, aside from the two women whispering to their friend.

I rose and walked towards Vincent, but he drew back from me and stayed away. So I just stood there with Vincent on one side of me and Hattori, Amelia and Alex on the other. I was still in shock. I could see that Herobrine was doing something on the other side of the room, no doubt working to achieve his aims.

The samurai turned his head towards me, his grey hair spread around him on the floor. He stretched out his hand in our direction and called to me and Vincent with a frail voice. 'Users . . .' he began.

I looked at Vincent, whose back was still turned. We couldn't let Hattori die without hearing what he wanted to say; he had a right to speak his last words. This was the very least I could do.

'Vincent,' I said. 'You need to pay attention.'

For a moment Vincent stayed where he was, but finally he gave in and turned. We walked slowly towards Hattori; every second and every step we took seemed to drag. Amelia turned to face Vincent as we kneeled by the samurai's side, but the priestess didn't seem to notice our presence. Hattori coughed, and we looked at one another quickly, feeling sure that he wasn't going to be able to say anything more.

He breathed heavily, staring at Vincent, and then he spoke. 'There's only one person to blame for what happened to me today . . . Herobrine.' He tightened his lips and a tear ran down his cheek. 'The User is aware of the damage he's done, and he's fought beside us to end Herobrine's tyranny. He sided with us, knowing this could lead to his death, and he's here now, in body and spirit, willing to correct his mistakes and help both our world and his own.'

With his free hand, Hattori stroked Alex's cheek.

'Find in your heart a place to forgive. You are a priestess,' he said.

Alex took a deep breath and then nodded, her blue eyes filled with tears.

I felt sick. What had I ever lost before now? A rabbit that had been run over a few years ago by a neighbour's car – although it had been terribly sad at the time, that was it. What did I have to compare to this kind of pain? I didn't know the meaning of loss, but I started to realize that I would never again see Hattori, that I would never again see my family and friends. Alex and Amelia would die too, and so would Vincent. There would be nothing left in the universe. Everything would be just a big black blur, like the Overworld's dead sky.

Hattori coughed again, then turned to me and Vincent. I listened carefully to every syllable.

'You must promise me you won't give up,' he said. 'The fight must go on. The world cannot be destroyed. We may never know the true meaning of the prophecies, or the reason why each of you was brought over here to our universe, Users . . . but we're bound together by ties to a much greater and a much longer battle: the struggle for survival. The struggle for freedom. The struggle to save everything dear to us. And this can never be done without making sacrifices.'

I nodded, tears running down my face.

'Vincent,' said Hattori, his voice barely a murmur now. 'You've already been in Herobrine's shoes. It takes a dictator to understand a dictator. He who knows his enemy . . .'

'. . . need not fear the result of a hundred battles,' Vincent finished.

Hattori smiled. And, at that, and without a sound . . . everything came to an end.

So that's it, I thought. *The end of a whole journey – of a whole life.*

Vincent and I rose to our feet while Alex and Amelia said goodbye to their friend. We stepped back and watched as his body turned into thousands of square pixels, which drifted away in the soft breeze blowing through the window. It was all over in just a few seconds.

I shook my head. We had to keep our wits about us and Hattori's death out of our minds for now, however hard that would be. Right then, most of all we had to make a move – we had to keep on fighting. There was this poem my father used to read me when I was a child – it talked about war and about having the courage to do impossible things in impossible situations.

> *Theirs not to make reply,*
> *Theirs not to reason why,*
> *Theirs but to do and die:*
> *Into the valley of Death*
> *Rode the six hundred.*

Yes, I would not fail. Just like Lord Tennyson wrote, I would do or die.

I lifted my sword and turned back to that creature from the Nether. He had moved away from us and was reading some sort of book. I looked at the enchantment table that stood in the centre of the library floor. The book that had lain on its surface before was now open in Herobrine's hands. And that book must have contained the secret of how to set the ender dragon free. I had to do something to stop him from achieving his goal and destroying both worlds.

'*Ph'nglui mglw'nafh,*' Herobrine began chanting, his hand raised over the pages of the book.

A strong wind began to blow. It was so powerful several books were blown off the shelves, and pens and paper flew all around the room. I was knocked backwards, and I had to cover my face to protect it from the objects flying through the air. Amelia and Alex were trying to get closer to Herobrine, but the wind made it impossible.

'*Herobrine Ender wgah'nagl fhtagn!*' Herobrine finished chanting his magic.

The wind blew stronger still, forcing me to shut my eyes. The tables were blown upside down. Alex and Amelia were shouting something, but I couldn't hear what they were saying. I felt as if I would be blown away – but then a hand grabbed my arm and pulled me towards the wall, where the wind wasn't as strong. I made an effort to open my eyes. Vincent pointed ahead, to where Herobrine was standing.

A giant portal had opened on the floor, and every block around it was being sucked inside. Herobrine laughed and threw the book into a corner of the library – he had no use for it now. The book was buffeted away by a gust of wind and ended up at our feet.

I thought I saw Vincent smile.

And then I understood why.

CHAPTER 23

THE ZOMBIE PIGMAN

Herobrine moved to the other side of the portal without even looking back at us. The wind dropped, leaving the room in total chaos, but the portal remained where it was, emitting a gurgling noise.

I swore. Heavy purple smoke began to billow from the open portal, and, in a flash, a zombie pigman emerged and stepped out into the library. The mob stood two metres tall; its pink flesh was decomposing, and through its open wounds I could see gristle and bones. I could smell the stench of its breath as the zombie pigman groaned, wielding a stick studded with iron spikes.

'Alex! Amelia!' Vincent called. 'I know what we need to do. Can you buy us some time?'

They nodded their heads and went up against our adversary. The monster pounded his chest and bellowed. The roar was neither human nor animal – it was purely monstrous.

'What are you saying?' I hissed.

Vincent crouched down on the floor and grabbed the book by our feet. I kneeled down next to him.

'The book,' he said. 'Do you remember what Hattori said?'

'About knowing your enemy?'

'That's right.' Vincent smiled. 'Herobrine's arrogance has led him to make a fatal error – a mistake I myself would have made when I was the Red King. It's very easy to be blind to what is obvious when you have so much power. Herobrine didn't even realize that he practically gave us the key to solving our problem . . . and causing his downfall.'

'The book?' I smiled. A shiver ran through my body, as though hope had reinvigorated me.

Vincent began flipping through the pages quickly. Close to the portal's edge, Alex and Amelia were still fighting against the undead mob.

'What is this book?' he asked, as though the answer would be obvious.

And, actually, it was obvious. I rubbed my forehead. The book was very different from the sort you usually found on enchantment tables. It was twice as big, for starters, and its pages were made of ancient parchment; it had a blue faded cover that was worn at the edges. The text written on its pages wasn't in the strange made-up symbols we'd seen on these books on the computer screen. I could read the words written in the book in front of us, but I didn't know what most of them meant.

'It's the prophecy book,' I said, and Vincent agreed.

I moved closer to him, trying to see the words as he flicked quickly through the pages.

'If we're right, this book could show us not only the way to fight against Herobrine, but also how to get back home,' Vincent said.

'What are we looking for?'

'I don't know. Any places where Users or Herobrine or the prophecy are mentioned . . .'

'Hang on!' I exclaimed. 'Just go back a bit.'

Vincent flipped back a few pages, but he was in such a hurry he could hardly turn them. I took the book from his hands and leafed back through the pages more slowly. I was sure I had seen the words 'portal' and 'Users' on the same page.

'Here!' said Vincent, putting his hand on one of the pages before I could turn it over.

We read the words together. There was a circle drawn in the centre of the page, and inside it was a sequence of ones and zeros, like the ones that had appeared in the sky when Herobrine had blotted out the daytime – like the ones I had seen before I'd been teleported into this world. At the top of the page, written in very clear letters, were the words USERS' PROGRAMMING MANUAL 101: POINT OF ORIGIN.

We stared at each other. It seemed to be an old-fashioned text, like a kind of tutorial, but it didn't make any sense. It involved blood, chanting some strange words, and drawing the symbol on the floor with the blood of whoever was doing the spell.

Still staring at one another, we nodded.

'It's now or never,' Vincent said.

He undid the strip of t-shirt cloth that was wrapped round his leg to protect his wound, and I did the same with the bandage on my injured hand, peeling it off in spite of the pain.

I rubbed the palm of my hand against the floor and then drew the symbol from the book with my blood. Vincent did the same with the blood from his leg, drawing each number inside the circle with his fingers so it exactly matched the book. Some numbers didn't come out very well, but we weren't going to be put off by that. Soon the drawing was ready. Then we held the book between us, staining its pages red with our blood, and began chanting the words together.

The same thing happened again: a windstorm, with gusts so strong it blew the furniture all round the room. The dust stung our eyes, but we carried on reading. I held down the pages as they thrashed in the wind, and lowered my face to the book so that I could see the words. We enacted the ritual exactly as it was written, repeating the phrases again and again, more and more loudly as the wind battered our faces. The zombie pigman let out a piercing squeal, as though he had been hit by something sharp.

Amelia and Alex held on to a nearby bookshelf and covered their eyes to protect themselves from the dust.

'I really hope this works!' Amelia yelled.

The windstorm began to subside, and the sound of lightning and a yellow glare filled the library. I looked in the direction of the noise, and I couldn't believe my eyes. There was a tear in reality there – a crease in the folds of time.

CHAPTER 24

REALITY TEAR

We were all blinded by the light. It was as if an atomic bomb had detonated right before our eyes. I blinked again and again as the flash of light shone, unable to see anything. A few seconds later, my vision returned and I rubbed my eyes repeatedly. Everything was blurred; I could see things that couldn't possibly be there. The tear in reality had ripped the world wide open, and, unless I had gone totally mad, I could see a very familiar scene.

On the other side of the world's veil, I saw my neighbours, Mallu and Arthur, sitting in front of a computer. They were both staring back at me, as astonished as I was. On their computer screen, a sequence of ones and zeros flashed on and on.

'Punk-Princess166 and Noobie Saibot,' said Vincent, with a little laugh. He seemed pleased, but at the same time upset by what he was seeing.

'Hang on a second,' I said, confused. 'Are *they* the legendary Users everyone talks about?'

'Yes,' Vincent said. 'They're just ordinary players like you and me. As time passed on this side, they turned into legends.'

I was going to say more, to tell Vincent there must be some mistake and they were just my neighbours, but I couldn't. Arthur and his sister were smiling, and, without hesitation, they stepped through the portal between the two worlds. The clothes they were wearing turned into blue armour. The portal behind them began to close, while pixels and fragments were pulled together in their hands, creating shining, razor-sharp diamond swords.

I couldn't believe my eyes. Mallu wielded her sword with total conviction and walked straight towards the zombie pigman, ripping him in two with a single blow. How could this be? She was my *neighbour*, the one who used to listen to loud music and argue with her brother – she *couldn't* be an Overworld legend! To begin with, I had no idea those two even played Minecraft. But, I reminded myself, whatever I thought was irrelevant – they were there, in front of me, and that was an indisputable fact.

All the excitement of the portal opening had come to an end, and my neighbours were greeting Amelia and Alex nostalgically, like friends who hadn't seen each other for a long time.

'I thought I'd never set foot here again!' said Mallu or, rather, Punk-Princess166 – Vincent had said that that was what she preferred to be called.

The priestess laughed happily.

'And we thought we would never see *you* again, kids,' said Amelia, who seemed delighted.

Alex and Amelia turned to me and Vincent.

'How did you do that?' asked Alex.

I was about to answer but then I noticed that there was a cold expression on the faces of the new arrivals, the Users. Vincent, who had remained silent, stared back at the two of them. I hoped there wasn't going to be a quarrel. Arthur walked towards us, stopping right in the spot where Hattori's body had lain before.

'To honour Hattori, I will leave you in peace,' said Arthur, with audible dislike.

'We haven't got time to waste with nonsense, avocado head,' his sister added, clearly referring to Vincent. 'We're going to *fight*.'

They didn't seem happy with Vincent, but, like me, they knew this wasn't the time to settle old scores. We had to work together if we were going to survive.

'Hang on a minute,' Alex said, hesitating. 'You know what happened to Hattori?'

'We do,' they answered in unison.

'All of this has been a big deal in the real world,' Punk-Princess166 said.

'Herobrine has already weakened the boundary that divides the two worlds to such an extent that players have now started seeing what's happening here,' Arthur explained, trying to give us some context. 'It happened little by little, you know? First the computer screen began flashing on and off, then your house disappeared around you, and then, all of a sudden, you could see the Overworld. It's been happening time and time again, involving more and more players. There are forums devoted solely to discussing this now. Most people think it's a publicity stunt, but Mallu and I knew the truth.'

'We've been trying to get back here for days.' Mallu turned to me. 'Time is synchronized between the two worlds now. Your parents have already called the police, Bia, and there are flyers with your photo everywhere.'

I felt something stir in my stomach; I thought I was going to be sick. I had no idea how I was going to explain all of this once I got back home. *Hey, Mum, I was inside a video game, fighting against a wicked dictator, you know what I mean . . .'* My mother would kill me. After lots of hugging and some tears at having found me, she would definitely kill me. I began thinking about her and my dad, and how worried they must have been. I silently promised I would be a better daughter once I got back, having meals at the right time and showing them how much I really cared.

It was Arthur's turn to speak. 'There are posters of your face all over school, Vincent.'

Vincent pursed his lips and raised a hand to his face. How much time had already passed since he had been drawn away from the real world?

'I don't think anyone is worried about my whereabouts,' he said. I searched his face. 'I haven't got time for this,' he continued. 'I must fight on.'

'Shut up, Vincent,' said Punk-Princess166. 'You better stop talking nonsense, otherwise I'm going to kick your butt so hard you'll *fly* back to reality.'

I was silent. Punk-Princess166 approached me and said, 'We'll have time to be sorry and mourn Hattori's death, to talk to our parents and sort it all out later, but now we have to find Herobrine. After all, what did Vincent once describe him as?'

'A bunch of useless pixels,' replied Arthur.

'That's it!' Punk-Princess166 had a smile on her face. 'Let's go after that bunch of useless pixels who thinks he's a big shot in the Minecraft world.'

And there we were, four Minecraft players united on a mission that could cost us a lot more than a few items and some experience points.

CHAPTER 25

NEW STRATEGY

The four of us had no time to talk about trivial things. Suddenly more monsters began appearing through the portal Herobrine had opened. That portal looked different from the ones that led to the End in the game. And, to make matters worse, all kinds of mobs had begun creeping up its sides, invading the library.

'We had some time to get ready before coming over,' said Punk-Princess166, fiddling in a pocket underneath her diamond armour. 'We were just waiting for the chance to get here.'

She looked like she'd found what she was looking for. She drew two little potion bottles from her pocket; I recognized them both. They were Potions of Healing. Confused, I wondered whether they would work here.

I quickly found out the answer – the minute Vincent and I drank the potions, our wounds healed and I was ready to go on fighting for another day.

As Alex and Amelia knocked down the first monsters to invade the library, Vincent showed the book to everyone.

'We can shut the portal again, but it may take a while,' he said.

I shook my head in disagreement. 'We can't afford to waste any more time,' I said. 'If you guys were watching all of this fighting from your homes, Herobrine must be close to blurring the boundaries of the two worlds together and destroying everything.'

'She's right,' said Alex, shooting an arrow at an enderman, and hitting it in the head.

'You have to go after him,' called Amelia, still fighting. 'I'll stay here and cover Alex while she shuts the portal.'

'But . . .'

Amelia cut me short. 'But you better be fast and

get back here before the portal is shut, otherwise you'll end up caught in there forever too.'

We looked at each other. This all seemed like total madness, but we knew we had to do it if we were going to keep our enemy trapped in the End. We had to seize this chance to put an end to it all, without running, without fleeing, without shortcuts. We were four Users against just one Herobrine – but what good would that be?

As if he could read my mind, Vincent said, 'We aren't going through the portal to defeat Herobrine.' His voice was calmer. 'That will be impossible now.'

'He's gone there to get the dragon,' Punk-Princess166 said, nodding in agreement. 'Our job is to make sure he can't get back, locking Herobrine and the dragon in the world's end forever.'

'The End wasn't a very nice place,' I said, remembering all the times I had gone there in the game.

It was just a vast area made up of end stone, packed with endermen and a dragon that flew over any player's head. Thinking about that place made my heart beat fast. This time I wouldn't be protected by a CPU or an avatar – I would be face to face with a nightmare. It would definitely be the worst journey of my life.

'We have to leave now, before it's too late,' Vincent said, looking at me. 'Ready?'

'I was born ready,' I replied, with a confidence I didn't really feel.

The four of us nodded and then ran towards the portal Herobrine had made, our swords in our hands, slaying every mob we came across on our way. My capacity for hope had been up and down in the past few days, like a see-saw that never stopped, and Herobrine always seemed a step ahead of us. But, as Vincent had said, Herobrine was proud – he was so arrogant he made silly mistakes, like leaving the book behind. He had no respect whatsoever for his enemies, so he had left us alive, entering the portal and leaving a few useless mobs to guard it.

I was ready to get back home, and I knew Vincent was too. We ran through the library. Punk-Princess166 and Arthur were the first ones to jump into the bubbling portal. I stood on its edge and I looked at Vincent beside me. I stretched out my hand and he took it. We bent over, fell forward, and let our bodies drop into the darkness.

About time.

ENDER DRAGON

By Punk-Princess166

The ender dragon, or end dragon, is called this because defeating it is one of the aims of Minecraft – if you can say that Minecraft has an aim.

The dragon is a sort of boss mob that appears in the End. It's a challenge to any player, whether they are skilled or not. The dimension where the dragon lives can only be accessed through one of the few portals there are in the Overworld. The End is mainly inhabited by hundreds of endermen.

The dragon (who is a female by the way) flies over the player's head, firing acid and swooping down. She kills a lot of players this way.

She is not the best companion to have around on a dark night.

Or right above your head.

CHAPTER 26

THE END

You might expect, given that I was already used to going through portals in Minecraft, that I wouldn't get sick doing it. But you'd be wrong. It was like at the theme parks I used to go to with my cousins: I was always the first person to get sick, which is why I was always last on to the rollercoaster.

The portal's distorted world came into focus before my eyes and, before I could look around, Vincent pushed my head so I was forced to look down. I stared at my filthy All Stars. The others looked down too, taking quick sidelong glances at each other's faces.

'They're everywhere,' said Arthur.

An enderman rubbed against my arm and I

170

shivered. I swallowed hard. How could we possibly walk through this crowd of endermen without getting killed?

'Has anybody got a pumpkin mask?' asked Vincent, looking uncomfortable after bumping into one of the mobs.

'There shouldn't be this many. Damn!' swore Punk-Princess166. 'What a mess!'

'We'll just have to walk looking down, or looking up at the sky,' I said.

'Looking up sounds like a better idea, given our situation,' Vincent said. 'And given that the dragon will fly over our heads soon.'

'What'll happen if we're hit by acid in this world?' asked Arthur.

'Nothing very nice, I imagine,' replied his sister. 'We have to carry on, we're running out of time.'

Behind us, we could see the blur that was the portal we had just come through. It seemed a little smaller now, but I hoped that was just a trick of my mind.

We walked together, keeping our heads down as we inched through the crowd of black arms and legs. The mobs teleported from one side to another with blasts and purple clouds, and every time I bumped into one I couldn't help starting. The floor was made of end stones, stretching out like an endless greenish sea.

I looked up over the endermen's heads and saw the black pillars holding the crystals that gave them life, which emitted a purplish glow.

As we got nearer to the centre of the plateau, we could hear the dragon's deafening roar.

It seriously gave me the creeps, and it seemed it did the same to my friends too. Nothing we had seen playing Minecraft could compare to that giant black dragon with its deep purple eyes.

The ground shook as the dragon roared again. And then it flapped its powerful wings and flew in our direction, ready to swoop down and strike us with its claws.

'Duck!' shouted Vincent, and I threw myself down, my nose flat on the ground.

The creature's leg flew a few centimetres above the skin of my back, and when I turned and looked behind me, there, riding on the dragon, was

Herobrine, wielding his sword and forcing the creature to turn back so that it could attack us again.

Lying next to me, Punk-Princess166 caught our attention. 'Remember – all we need to do is buy some time. Don't take any unnecessary risks, OK?'

I nodded, stretching out my arms and legs a bit as I lay there.

'Who looks more tasty? Me and Vincent?' I asked. 'Or Mallu and Arthur?'

'Punk-Princess166!' she shouted, outraged. 'And Noobie Saibot! I didn't come to this world to be called by my birth name.'

We put the debate aside and ran. Vincent and I went to one side and Noobie and Punk-Princess166 went to the other, trying to confuse the dragon, which landed on the ground in the spot where we had been just a few moments before.

I ran towards the columns and put my back against the obsidian, next to Vincent. In the distance I saw our friends do the same.

'We're like ducks on a lake – totally unprotected,' said Vincent, sneaking a quick look from behind the column.

The dragon roared, frustrated at not being able to bite its victims.

'What do we do?' I asked. 'We can't just keep running back and forth. Herobrine's going to get to us at some point.'

Herobrine seemed amused, unaware that he was wasting precious time.

'What if we killed an enderman?' I suggested.

Vincent stared at me doubtfully.

'Just think,' I went on insistently. 'We can use its ender pearl to teleport from one place to another, so if the dragon gets close to us, at least we can flee quickly.'

Vincent agreed then, and lifted his sword.

I heard an enderman's shriek, then the dragon's roar. What was happening?

An enderman wandered by absently, and I stabbed it with all my might, my sword aiming for its head.

My blade pierced the creature's neck, and it staggered. I hung on to the sword's hilt, and Vincent struck the enderman on its knees, forcing it to fall, and giving me the chance to thrust the sword deeper and finish the mob once and for all.

Quickly, Vincent cut the enderman's chest open and plucked out a big pearl, covered in the goo of its blood.

Our fight had caught the dragon's eye; it trotted towards us. Herobrine, on its back, shouted, 'Finish them off – now!'

I stretched out my hand and grabbed the pearl. In an instant we were standing next to another column, right in front of Punk-Princess166 and Noobie Saibot, who were gasping for breath as though they'd been running. Near by there was a puddle of acid burning into the floor.

'You distracted the dragon just in time,' said Noobie Saibot, showing me that he had a pearl too.

The dragon was sniffing the ground, then it leaped, flapping its heavy wings as it flew over the plateau. We didn't have long – we would be discovered soon.

Punk-Princess166 fumbled in her pockets, then drew out some more potion bottles and an enchanted bow.

'How did you do that?' I asked, surprised. 'It looks like you've got a whole inventory in there!'

She smiled. 'I told you I'd prepared for this

moment. I made sure the character I played was fully equipped, and it looks as if I brought everything over here with me.'

'Don't get so overexcited, princess,' said Vincent. 'This only means that the veil that divides the two worlds is even more fragile than it was before.'

'Stop being such a killjoy. So what if it means something bad – if we can take advantage of the opportunity, why shouldn't we?'

'All the world's players must be watching us now,' said Noobie Saibot. He winced briefly as the dragon let out an ear-piercing roar.

I took a deep breath in. 'I only hope they realize this isn't just a game,' I said, looking around and wondering whether I really was being watched by thousands of people. 'Hang on. If they're watching, and if you can interact with the real world, reaching for your Minecraft inventory . . . would it be possible for them to do the same?'

'You mean, to get here?' asked Vincent.

'I don't know,' I replied. 'But if they could use a cheat and enable Peaceful mode, that would be very useful.'

Punk-Princess166 smiled. 'It's easy to dream!' she said.

Our talk was interrupted by the sight of claws wrapping around the column we were hidden behind. Punk-Princess166 handed out the bottles she had in her hands, and we all drank them quickly.

They were Potions of Swiftness. Each of us ran in opposite directions, faster than the dragon. Punk-Princess166 took advantage of the fact that the monster was distracted and hit it with several arrows. I knew the arrows weren't really going to hurt the dragon, as the crystals were still shining brightly above the pillars, but they helped to keep it busy.

Noobie moved to stand with his sister, his sword in his hand, and struck the dragon's body hard, making it shriek.

Herobrine did not look happy.

The dragon's tail swung hard, hitting both brother and sister and flinging them across the plateau. Then the dragon flew high. I just about managed to avoid being hit by the acid cloud it breathed at me before it flew away.

'For how long will we have to distract them?'

asked Vincent, watching Punk-Princess166 and Noobie Saibot as they got up off the floor and ran to hide behind one of the pillars again.

'I don't think Herobrine cares about us,' I replied. Herobrine was laughing and boasting about having such a powerful dragon under his control. 'He just thinks we're trying to slay him. He has no idea that all we want to do right now is buy time.'

'If we want to keep it that way, then we need to look more convincing,' Vincent said.

'I know. But how do we do that without getting killed?'

Vincent looked up, pointing to the crystals at the top of the pillar.

'By not attacking the dragon,' he answered. 'Come with me.'

Of course! If we attacked the crystals, we could keep ourselves at a safe distance from the dragon without looking as though we were just killing time.

We both ran, taking advantage of the effects of the Potion of Swiftness to get to the place where the siblings were standing.

THE END

Noobie Saibot's face was covered in scratches from his fall, and Punk-Princess166 did not look happy.

The battle had just begun.

CHAPTER 27

LIVE STREAM

Punk-Princess166 broke into a run, darting round each pillar while we kept the dragon distracted by attacking it with calculated strikes, always keeping a safe distance away.

Herobrine was laughing as though the battle had already been won. 'I gave you a chance to live in your world in peace for a few more days,' he said from high above, standing up on the dragon's back. 'But you chose to come back here and die at my own hand!'

'That's where you're wrong, you idiot,' shouted Punk-Princess166, hitting one of the crystals with an arrow.

The crystal exploded. The dragon seemed to have

felt the impact; it turned and ran at Punk-Princess166, snorting, ready to fire an acid cloud.

'Run!' I shouted.

I tried to catch the dragon's attention, but it ignored me, far more intent on Punk-Princess166, who had destroyed the crystal.

Noobie Saibot and Vincent ran together, striking the dragon's back with their swords. The creature flew into the air, but then it spun round fast and hit both of them with one of its wings. Punk-Princess166, filled with rage, rained down arrows on her enemy.

Herobrine jumped on to the ground and walked straight towards me, staring at me disdainfully. I clenched my fists, knowing I stood no chance against him. There, behind Herobrine, Vincent was trapped against the wall as the dragon took a deep breath, ready to attack him.

It seemed appropriate for us to meet our end there, in the End.

Herobrine signalled and several endermen began to charge, even though we weren't looking at them. Punk-Princess166 beheaded one of them and struck another, but she was outnumbered, and in the end she took a blow to her stomach and then her face.

Noobie Saibot was screaming, charging at the dragon, but the mob was bent on finishing off Vincent, who was frozen to the spot and staring at it with dread in his eyes.

'Look at your friends, girl,' Herobrine said to me. 'Know that all of them will be slain because of me, and that soon your world and every creature, be they mobs or humans, will meet the same fate.'

'Do you *really* think we're going to let you get away with this?' I said.

He smiled scornfully. 'As if you have what it would take to stop me. This battle here? It's a joke. A way for me to practise riding the dragon, and nothing more.'

Punk-Princess166 disappeared using one of the pearls. I saw her out of the corner of my eye, rescuing Vincent right at the last second. A giant purple acid cloud was burning into the wall where he had stood. Herobrine didn't seem to notice.

'Do you know what your problem is, Nether

ghost?' I asked, smiling, knowing that what I was about to say would anger him. 'You have no idea what we are capable of. Every block you walk on, every pixel you were made with, was created by us.'

I relaxed a bit now that I knew my friends were safe from the dragon. I walked a few steps away from Herobrine. I didn't want to talk to him any more – I wanted to talk to all those people who were watching us. It was hard to believe that they couldn't reach us. I could feel the Red King's and Herobrine's impact in the real world. We could all feel it – the destruction of biomes, maps and entire servers. It was like a virus affecting both worlds.

I looked up. 'What you're watching now isn't an ad campaign. What you're seeing now is real. Hattori? He's really dead!' I took a deep breath. 'Us?' I pointed at my own chest. 'We're really here, and each and every wound, every breath we take, and every word we say is as real as the screen you're looking at now. How many of you have had your constructions destroyed by the Red King? How many of you have woken up one day to find the entire world you had created had vanished from the server? How many of you can recognize my face, or the faces of my friends?'

With a click, Vincent, Noobie Saibot and Punk-Princess166 appeared by my side. They looked up so that their faces could be seen too.

'We need all the help we can get,' said Noobie Saibot. He had a large cut across his face now.

'What kind of players are you, if you just stay there, looking?' Punk-Princess166 shouted.

'If he can hurt you,' Vincent said, pointing to Herobrine, 'if *I* could hurt you when I was the Red King, you are able to strike back. You can reach us!'

There was a long silence.

The dragon stopped flapping its wings and alighted on the ground.

The endermen stopped screaming and laughing. They swayed their arms but their legs were still.

We held our breath for fear of what would happen next. Herobrine, standing in front of us, gave a low laugh full of disdain.

Something white appeared in my field of vision. I looked down and to the left, smiling broadly at what I saw. There was a message written in square white letters.

The letters floated in the atmosphere, crystal clear.

/DIFFICULTY 0

The message was repeated again and again, through the whole dimension, floating in the air all around us.

Those players who had been watching us had used a cheat on their computers, and it was affecting the Overworld. The game had been modified to difficulty zero and Peaceful mode had been enabled, so all the endermen around us began to disappear one by one.

Herobrine roared with rage, pointing his sword at us. We ran away, trying to escape.

Then another message appeared right before my eyes.

Zombie_Master: Bia, I've been following you for a few days – don't die now like a bunch of noobs.

'Ah! Shut up!' I shouted, but I couldn't help smiling.

The messages began to appear everywhere – on the floor, on the columns, on the dragon, over Herobrine's head and in the air around us.

Nether's ghost screamed, trying to grab the messages, but they couldn't be touched.

Tommie_VIP: Vincent, we don't care if you destroyed our entire server, as long as you FINISH OFF HEROBRINE.

Love-CAT: PLEASE, don't give up, this is my world and my favourite game too!

Honey-pandaBear45: Get back to our planet!

JudieCorn: You have no idea how lucky you are to be inside the game! You MUST save our favourite game!

MARI_Chan: I KNOW you'll make it!

Rainbow-SIX: Fighting against him looks scary, but do it for us, for you, for everyone!

CLOUDY_bird: PUNK-PRINCESS166, PLEASE, GIVE ME YOUR EMAIL <3

LukeLuke: GO FOR IT!

QueenBee: We believe in you, Users!

The four of us reunited, swords in our fists. New messages appeared before us, and the spectators started using more cheats so new swords appeared in our hands, shining with the glow of enchantment. And the same happened to our bodies, until I found myself completely protected by shining armour.

I could run faster, jump higher, and my arms were more powerful. I thanked all of those players in my mind for their messages of support and for believing in us. Then, with a cry of victory, the four of us charged at Herobrine, who shrank back in pain as we struck him.

'I'm going to slay all of you,' he shouted, but the messages kept coming.

As my sword clashed against his, I realized I was no longer a weak girl fighting against a monster. I deftly kicked him in the chest, pushing him away and striking once again. Herobrine was being forced back, swearing as we became stronger thanks to the codes typed by the players who were watching us.

Vincent was wearing red armour and his sword looked like it was made up of rubies, but if he noticed the references to his past, it didn't seem to bother him.

Punk-Princess166 and Noobie Saibot kept fighting against the dragon, which was struggling now as it was pelted with arrows and snowballs. Someone seemed to have given the siblings some TNT, and both of them were running to hurl it at the dragon.

The blast echoed all around us, opening a massive wound in the creature's chest. But we were running out of time – there, far away, the portal was fading. I only realized the danger when messages of warning began to appear.

SiLvInHa: YOU HAVE TO RUN!!!

Zero-Zero: FAST!

Mermaid-Lider: GO NOW!

The messages made us hurry, but they also made Herobrine realize what our plan was, so that even though he was badly injured with a wound to his chest, he chased after us.

The messages encouraged us to run, and our

enchanted boots meant that we could sprint faster than Herobrine. Just as I was reaching the portal, which was already closing, I heard a piercing scream. I looked back and Noobie Saibot and Punk-Princess166 stopped beside me.

Dinosaur_King: No!!!

Fans-of-Vincent: Bite him!

Bunny-Pie: Vincent!!!11!

RedQueen: Can you get away, please!!

I ignored the messages that appeared around me. There, behind us, Herobrine had caught Vincent and he had him trapped, with the sword pointed at his neck.

'You're going to stop the portal from closing *right now*!' he roared.

Herobrine knew he stood no chance against the four of us when all the other world's players were on our side too.

I frowned, grabbing my sword with my right hand and holding out my left. 'Another sword,' I said.

In a split second, an extra sword appeared in my left hand.

'Teleport,' I said next.

Messages appeared with the command for me to teleport over Herobrine, and, in a second, I was there, stabbing him from behind.

Vincent broke loose and grabbed my hand; we ran as fast as we could, with Punk-Princess166 and Noobie Saibot on our tail. A white scratch was all that was left of the portal now. We jumped into it and I felt something yanking me from the centre of my body.

Everything spun around me, and then, finally, my feet landed on the library's wooden floor.

Herobrine was imprisoned in the world's end forever.

LIFE AFTER THE BATTLE

USERS UNITED

We were back. We lay there on the floor, injured, tired and dirty, but completely and absolutely relieved. Herobrine was imprisoned in the End, and the Overworld could finally start to heal. When most people would have given up and thrown in the towel, we had carried on, despite everything, despite the losses we had suffered.

Alex and Amelia finished off a few remaining monsters, then they ran towards us, giving all of us a big hug.

'We got lucky,' Noobie said. 'We finally managed to kick that jerk's butt. We ran out of time to do it the last time we were here.'

'Yeah,' said Punk-Princess166. 'He realized we

were about to shut those shining eyes of his for good, and he sent us back to the real world, just when I had started to get used to this place.'

I smiled as Vincent approached, his hands in his pockets.

'I know what's going to happen now,' he said enigmatically. 'If my calculations were right, that is.'

The other Users looked askance at my travel companion.

'What are you talking about, melon head?' Punk-Princess166 asked.

Vincent smiled. 'I did something when I was summoning you,' he said. 'Pay attention, because –'

He didn't get the chance to finish his sentence – he was cut off by the sound of thunder and a red glow sweeping through the library. I closed my eyes for a moment, then opened them slowly, as though I was bracing myself to see a monster spawning before my eyes. But what I saw was the opposite. There was light, lots of it, on every side. The everlasting night had departed, and the remaining monsters were burning up under the powerful sun.

'How did you do that?' I asked. 'I was sure that

Herobrine had destroyed the Overworld forever!'

Amelia burst out laughing. 'You restarted the world and made the sun appear, didn't you?' she said. 'Mate, I'm almost sorry I didn't trust you.'

'It's fine. I wouldn't have trusted myself either if I'd been in your shoes,' Vincent replied, and then he stretched out on the floor, finally taking a rest. 'Wake me up next year, or the year after that,' he said.

There was quiet. The voices of the hundreds of players had been silenced, monsters had been burned, and there we were, alone in the centre of the library. A part of me felt like imitating Vincent, but, as if he had read my thoughts, Noobie spoke.

'Unfortunately,' he said, 'I don't think that's going to be possible. Our mission has ended here, so we need to get back home. Whenever Users stay here for too long, strange things happen.'

I looked at him, knowing he was right, but not knowing how to say goodbye to those people I had met here – to Hattori Hanzō, who had died, and to all those who had fought beside me. For a reason I couldn't explain, and totally against my will, tears began to run down my face.

'Don't cry, Bia,' said Alex. 'There is peace in the Overworld now thanks to you and your friends. Don't regret having come to the end, but treasure this journey you have shared with us. As long as you carry this world inside you, we will be together.'

'Yeah,' said Punk-Princess166. 'You even have the chance to say your goodbyes. Last time Herobrine sent us away before we could even say the *word* "bye".'

I wiped my tears away and nodded. I would never forget this world. I would never forget a single detail.

Arthur approached us, with the prophecy book opened on a particular page. 'We have to get back home,' he said. 'Our worlds are still synchronized, so we can't stay here for too long.'

Alex held the book while all of us Users gathered round. We said our goodbyes as quickly as we could, and Amelia gave me a piece of redstone.

'Just a souvenir,' she said, 'that's all.' She gave a piece to each of the others and gave everyone a hug, and then Alex hugged everyone too. When she got to Vincent she whispered something in his ear – whatever it was, it made him smile and nod his head.

'I need you to hold each other's hands,' said the priestess. 'I don't want any of you getting lost between one world and the other.'

We did as we were told, holding each other's hands; I was stood between Vincent and Arthur. Alex began reciting the words from the book, gesturing with her hands. I could tell it was working – my fingers tingled, and we were being enveloped by a blue light.

'I have nothing waiting for me on the other side,' said Vincent. 'Absolutely nothing.'

'Don't be such an idiot,' I said. 'We're the Users who saved the Overworld – we've got each other.'

'You won't be able to get rid of us that easily, you moron,' Punk-Princess166 added.

We all laughed. Our mission in the Overworld had come to an end, but we knew there was something even more amazing in store for us on the other side.

A lifetime.

The End

EXTRAS: BEYOND THE OVERWORLD

INTERVIEW: HEROBRINE

Hello! Today we managed to interview the biggest celebrity of all time. His name is Herobrine, and he makes a lot of noise everywhere he goes, in both the literal and figurative senses. This interview took a great deal of negotiation and several months to be arranged – after all, destroying every world is a task that is bound to take up a lot of time. I do hope you enjoy our interview.

Q: Hello, Herobrine. It's a pleasure to meet you. Can you talk a bit about you and your future plans?
Herobrine: What do you mean? Is there still someone who doesn't know who I am? Just tell me who this person is and I will devour their soul and

roast their flesh in the fire of the Nether. I am Herobrine, the conqueror, the destroyer of every world, Nether's ghost, the spectre that walks the earth.

Q: Sure. Umm. Can you talk a bit about your childhood?

H: My childhood? Yes . . . I had a good childhood. I used to torment creepers, endermen and zombies for hours on end. It was a very happy childhood.

Q: You used to torment zombies?

H: I did . . . when I conquer the world, all school children will learn how to destroy planets, play pranks and burp after they've eaten lunch.

Q: Don't you think that hurting classmates and zombies is cruel?

H: Have you got some kind of issue with that? I would be more than happy to use you as a guinea pig instead . . .

Q: Umm . . . I think we'd better change the subject. What's your favourite band?

H: That's easy. I love Creeper Cannibal, a rock band who write beautiful lyrics. My favourite tune is from the *Enderman Empire* record, and it's called 'I Destroyed Your Crops and Your Mines'. A real hit!

Q: OK, now let's play a game – I'll say a few words and you just tell me the first thing that comes into your head. Let's kick off with the first word: happiness.

H: My enemies weeping or mourning.

Q: A happy day.

H: The day I drove the Users out of this world and began large-scale destruction.

Q: A dream.

H: Having a photo taken with the guys from Creeper Cannibal; they're my idols and inspire me a lot.

Q: A perfect place.

H: Any place that's destroyed and filled with fire. Somewhere cool and comfortable, like the Nether.

Q: That's great. Herobrine, I'd like to thank you for giving us the opportunity to interview you. I'm sure *Steve Magazine* readers will love your story.

H: I am the one who should be thanking you for giving me the chance to show that a Lord of Evil can be nice when he isn't destroying your house or your life. Thank you very much. Just one more thing – make me look cool in your article, otherwise I will lock you in a basement in the Nether and that will be the end of you.

Q: Sure, I will, Herobrine – I'll make sure everyone knows that you're the coolest and most amazing guy I've ever met.

H: I hope so. For your sake . . .

ACKNOWLEDGEMENTS

It has been a long journey up to this point – as long as the journey my characters have taken. I would like to thank a lot of people who helped me, supported me and followed my work (and all the crying on the internet).

First of all: thank you, readers. Without you, I would not be here today. Without the thousands of readers of *The Sword of Herobrine*, it would have been impossible to continue this journey. Thank you! You rock!

Thank you to my wife (for putting up with me and for everything else) and to my cat (January, the First One with This Name, Queen of the Seven Sand Boxes, Fan of Cat Sachets).

Thank you to my old friends, for listening to me for hours as I told them my ideas, and for forgiving me when I borrowed their CDs and didn't give them back. I would also like to thank my new friends, for listening to me when I spent hours telling them about my ideas, and for forgiving me when I borrowed their CDs and didn't give them back.

Thank you to the musicians whose music helped me work until the late hours of the night – you're amazing!

Thank you, Eiichiro Oda, for creating *One Piece*, *Tite Kubo*, for *Bleach*, and the CLAMP ladies, for everything you did (I mean it, I love it all).

Thank you, my friends from abroad. You guys, thank you: Baz, Insuni, Darren, Ben, Alejandra, Charlie, Laura. Hey, we need a party.

Thank you, Eduardo, Carol, Marcelo and Arnaud, for putting up with me and making this story possible. All the production and editing teams. You are bold and brave . . . I am grateful! Thank you to everyone at Grupo Autêntica publishing house, you are awesome. As the master says: it's us.

And if I have forgotten anyone, please, forgive

me. At times memory fails me, sometimes long working hours, and, other times, watching serials or reading. If you are a cool person, then I am thanking you too.

Hugs,
Jim

KEEP CALM
AND
PLAY
MINECRAFT

OUT NOW

When a mysterious code sucks Arthur's Minecraft-obsessed sister into the Overworld, Arthur has no choice but to follow her. The siblings must battle zombies, dodge creepers, and do whatever it takes to survive.

As they travel through the Overworld, it becomes clear that their only real hope is tied to an ancient legend. A legend about the very worst creature in the world of the game.

His name?

HEROBRINE.

 **Listen**

Do you love listening to stories?

Want to know what happens behind the scenes in a recording studio?

Hear funny sound effects, exclusive author interviews and the best books read by famous authors and actors on the **Puffin Podcast** at **www.puffin.co.uk**

#ListenWithPuffin

Your story starts here . . .

Do you **love books** and **discovering new stories**? Then **www.puffin.co.uk** is the place for you . . .

- Thrilling adventures, fantastic fiction and laugh-out-loud fun

- Brilliant videos featuring your favourite authors and characters

- Exciting competitions, news, activities, the Puffin blog and SO MUCH more . . .

It all started with a Scarecrow

Puffin is over seventy years old.
Sounds ancient, doesn't it? But Puffin has never been
so lively. We're always on the lookout for the next big
idea, which is how it began all those years ago.

Penguin Books was a big idea from the mind of
a man called Allen Lane, who in 1935 invented
the quality paperback and changed the world.
**And from great Penguins, great Puffins grew,
changing the face of children's books forever.**

The first four Puffin Picture Books were hatched in 1940 and the
first Puffin story book featured a man with broomstick arms called
Worzel Gummidge. In 1967 Kaye Webb, Puffin Editor, started the
Puffin Club, promising to **'make children into readers'**.
She kept that promise and over 200,000 children became devoted
Puffineers through their quarterly instalments of *Puffin Post*.

Many years from now, we hope you'll look back and
remember Puffin with a smile. **No matter what your age
or what you're into, there's a Puffin for everyone.**
The possibilities are endless, but one thing is for sure:
whether it's a picture book or a paperback, a sticker book
or a hardback, **if it's got that little Puffin
on it – it's bound to be good.**